The Naked Eye

The Naked Eye

Yoko Tawada

Translated from the German by SUSAN BERNOFSKY

A NEW DIRECTIONS BOOK

An excerpt from *The Naked Eye* first appeared in the journal *Two Lines*.

Manufactured in the United States of America

First published as New Directions Paperbook (NDP1139) in 2009

Library of Congress Cataloging-in-Publication Data
Tawada, Yoko, 1960–
[Das nackte Auge. English]
The Naked Eye / Yoko Tawada ; translated from the German
by Susan Bernofsky.
p. cm.
ISBN 978-0-8112-1739-2 (pbk.: acid-free paper)
I. Bernofsky, Susan. II. Title.
PT2682.A87N3313 2009
895.6'35—dc22   2009000610

10 9 8 7 6 5 4

New Directions Books are published for James Laughlin
by New Directions Publishing Corporation
80 Eighth Avenue, New York 10011

for C. D.

Translator's Note

The Naked Eye is Yoko Tawada's first truly bilingual book, a departure from her usual practice of writing in either German or Japanese and then giving the text to a translator. She started the novel in German, but then parts of the story began occurring to her in Japanese, and so she continued writing sections of the book now in one language, now in the other, later translating in both directions until she arrived simultaneously at two complete manuscripts. The linguistic indeterminacy of this process beautifully reflects the situation of the novel's narrator, a young Vietnamese woman who is multiply displaced and tends to speak in declarative sentences as if desperate to pin down a world that keeps shifting around her. The present translation is based solely on the German version of the novel.

—Susan Bernofsky

The Naked Eye

Chapter One

Repulsion

An eye on film, affixed to an unconscious body. The eye sees nothing for the camera has already robbed it of vision. The gaze of the nameless lens licks the floor like a detective without grammar. A doll, another doll, a stuffed animal, a vase, cacti, a television, electrical cords, a basket, the corner of a sofa, a bit of rug, tea-biscuit crumbs, sugar cubes, an old family photograph. The photograph shows a girl looking up and to the side; there's nothing there. The girl's one eye grows larger and larger as the focus changes, more and more blurred—now it resembles a speck on a sheet of paper. Who will be able to guess, later on, that this speck was once an eye? The camera slowly retreats. Beside an overturned sofa, a cabinet is standing upside-down. It isn't possible to reconstruct a story from this landscape of ruins.

In this film I saw you for the first time. One year before, I was attending high school in Ho Chi Minh City, formerly known as Saigon, which was often still referred to by this name. In the eyes of the teachers, I was the pupil with the iron blouse. My grades were unrivalled. That spring our school received a letter from the German Democratic Republic inviting us to send one student to an International Youth Conference to be held in Berlin. The organizers were hoping to hear an authentic report on the topic "Vietnam As a Victim of American Imperialism." The principal of our school had good contacts in the GDR and had been there himself. He'd told us several times about his visit to Berlin and a certain "Pergamon Museum." "Pergamon" sounded like the name of a migratory bird, and it amused us to picture the Berlin skies with this bird flapping around in them. The teachers held a special meeting and ended up choosing me. The essays I wrote were generally lucid, and I also had the voice of a crane, which was why I'd often been chosen to speak at sports festivals or receptions for official visitors. Besides, I probably gave the impression of being difficult to seduce.

It was my first time on an airplane. I was looking forward to the trip, and it never occurred to me that I might be in any danger. But as the faces of my family and friends who'd brought me to the airport were slightly distorted with fear, I began to feel concerned. Maybe there was something they'd hidden from me so I wouldn't be scared. But what could it be? I had no idea how the mechanism of an airplane functioned, but I was nonetheless convinced that my airplane was in perfect working order. I had never before set foot in such a large, hard, spotlessly clean vehicle. My older brother's motorcycle, for example, was nothing but a rusty ox full of dents and scratches. Who knew if it still had all its screws. Compared to this motorcycle the Interflug airplane, which no doubt had "Made in Germany" stamped on it somewhere, appeared to me completely trustworthy.

After I fastened my seatbelt and pulled it snug, I felt a great sense of relief. From this point on, anything that might happen would no longer be my responsibility. I drank my ration of water and fell asleep. Now and then I felt the cold window pressing against my left temple and woke up.

In Berlin I was met by two young men. At first I was a bit surprised because they looked just like Americans. But then they greeted me in Russian, which was reassuring.

"Welcome! How was your journey with our Interflug?"
One of them took my suitcase from me. He appeared
to be rather horrified, no doubt because it was unexpectedly light. The other one was trying to insert his index
and middle fingers into the front pocket of his jeans, but
in reality there was no pocket. At the same time, he was
looking at the buttons of my white blouse. When our eyes
met, he grinned. In certain streets in Saigon there were ill-
mannered youths who grinned like this. They wore jeans
manufactured in Thailand or the GDR and spent the whole
day observing the passersby instead of going to work. I
wondered whether this man really was a Party member.
Our eyes met once more, and this time he smiled in a more
respectable way.

Berlin was an enormous trade show of old palaces. If a
sort of inflation exists that applies to ruins, it must look
something like this. Such magnificent buildings repeated
over and over ad nauseum look ostentatious and discon-
nected. Despite the grandeur of its architecture, though,
the city couldn't be prosperous, for there were no delicacies
anywhere on the streets: no stands selling noodle soup, no
fruit markets or coconut vendors. You couldn't smell any
food at all. My uncle had said to me before my departure:
"Too bad you aren't going to Hungary or Czechoslovakia.
Bulgaria would have been tasty, too. But Germany!" At first
I was somewhat aggrieved to hear these words from my

flippant uncle, yet perhaps he was right. The Hungarians and Czechs, he explained, knew how to produce good peppers and were excellent cooks. And in Bulgaria you could not only eat good cucumbers, tomatoes, and yoghurt, you also had your choice of excellent hot and cold springs for bathing. My uncle owned a fat, brown Czech motorcycle that he'd bought from the army and repaired himself. He polished it regularly and was quite proud of it. My older brother, however, would say disparagingly to his friends: "Just look! It's our uncle's fat Czech Buddha!" My uncle in turn despised the old, tiny Honda moped my brother had bought secondhand at the market. He thought it was effeminate.

My talk was scheduled for the following day. I was then invited to spend another five nights at the hotel. I had never seen such a gigantic hotel. It was like a beehive with innumerable windows—from the outside you couldn't tell if the windows were open or shut. I remembered a different uncle who'd studied agricultural technology here and then died soon after returning home. Next to the hotel, an enormous statue of an onion blossom rose into the air. The sphere at its tip gleamed like the roof of a Thai temple. "This tower is forty-four meters higher than the Eiffel Tower," said one of my young hosts. And the other added, laughing: "But its root is short." "Have you ever been to Paris?" I asked. Both of them shook their heads from side to side in unison. Then all three of us burst out laughing without knowing why.

The woman working at the hotel's reception desk looked like the principal of a school. While giving me the key she explained something in German which one of the two men immediately translated into Russian for me. "A Russian rock band will be performing tonight at the hotel restaurant. Free of charge. Perhaps you'd like to go." He pointed down the dim corridor where the restaurant was apparently located. Then we arranged to meet the following day. My chaperones wanted to pick me up at the hotel at nine in the morning and bring me to the conference site. I was hungry. As soon as the two of them had disappeared through the hotel's front door, I hurried to the restaurant. It was still closed. "Opening times 6:00 – 10:00 p.m." Even a luxurious hotel restaurant here couldn't afford to serve meals for more than four hours a day. The distribution of foodstuffs in this country seemed not to be functioning optimally. I went to my room, which looked tidy, swept, mopped, and polished. It smelled of unfamiliar chemicals.

I took my manuscript out of my suitcase. Although I had practiced with my Russian teacher every day for a week reading my essay aloud, suddenly I couldn't remember a single line of it. I read the whole thing aloud to myself once through. In a foreign country, even my own handwriting looked questionable.

•

At exactly six I left my room to go to the restaurant. The door to the restaurant was no longer locked, but there wasn't a single customer inside. After a while an ill-humored waiter brought me a bilingual menu, Russian and German. He never returned so I got up and went to the kitchen to look for him. Among the large shiny silver pots and vessels I saw the waiter reading a magazine. "I would like to order soup and a salad," I said in Russian. "We have such things *nyet*." "So what do you have?" "Steak." "I don't want to eat meat. Can I order just potatoes?" The waiter got up and disappeared out back. I wasn't sure whether to read this as hope or resignation with regard to the potatoes.

A man with narrow hips who looked like a sailor appeared on the stage and began tuning his electric guitar. He was wearing green bellbottoms and a tight, frivolously shiny polyester shirt with a sunflower pattern. He stamped his feet, possibly to keep the cables that were lying on the stage like a family of snakes from wrapping around his legs. His shoes were narrow, pointed and the same shade of white as the sweet tofu served for dessert in China. Yet another black-haired musician appeared. He looked exactly like Nikita from my illustrated language textbook. "Is Nikita home?" "No, he is not home." So where has Nikita gone if he's no longer at home? Did he go to Germany like me? "When is he coming home?" "I don't know." The practice sentences from my textbook were slipping back into my head. I always got good grades in Russian, but there was one grammatical rule to which I had a physical aversion: the genitive of negation. A person who was absent was no longer allowed to exist in the nominative case, as though he were no longer a subject.

There still wasn't a single other guest in the restaurant. Nikita was glancing about absent-mindedly, and one of his glances swept past me. I was only a piece of furniture like a chair or table. Yet another man in a brown shirt came on stage and put his electric bass under his arm. My little brother would have been excited to see this concert. He once tore down the poster of Sputnik our father had given him and in its place put up a poster of a sweaty rock band posing beneath a colorful shower of lights.

The musicians finished their sound check and went backstage. My potatoes still didn't come. Perhaps they, too, had already been transformed into the inedible genitive on account of their absence.

The restaurant seemed strangely familiar. It resembled a government reception hall in Saigon. If it hadn't been for the absence of food, I'd almost have felt at home. Soon a large group of Russian tourists sat down, and an air of merriment filled the room.

The potatoes still didn't come. Instead of the waiter, a reindeer appeared before me. The reindeer was knitted into the sweater of a young man whose blond hair grew down to his shoulders. "May I join you?" he asked me in Russian with an unusual accent. I'd scarcely nodded before he was

Yoko Tawada

sitting beside me. "Where are you from?" He was using the familiar form of address even though we didn't yet know each other. "Vietnam." He gave a downy smile and replied that he was from Bochum. I hadn't even asked where he was from, and I'd never before heard the name "Bochum." It sounded more like a cough than the name of a town. "Is Bochum near Berlin?" "Around six hours by train, I think." "That means it's on the Czech border." "No, the closest border is Holland, I think." Of course I knew there was a country called Holland, but the map of Europe in my head was full of blank spots. I could see Russia and Poland clearly, but everything that lay to the west of Berlin was blurry because a sandy desert wind was blowing there. France, too, had to be somewhere. That country had enjoyed our hospitality for a while and therefore was covered in history classes. My great-grandparents on my mother's side supposedly spoke French, and my mother and several of my school friends felt a vague longing for this country.

The young man ordered vodka for us. I had never before drunk wine, but I'd tried vodka a few times already because my father brought some home now and then as a gift from the Party. Once he showed us the label on the vodka bottle and remarked: "The ending of Stolichnaya is feminine, just like the ending of Moskovskaya." "Why are they feminine?" "Because vodka is feminine." "Does it never happen that vodka is given a masculine name?" "Once. The Gorbachev family, who fled to Berlin in 1921 during the revolution, manufactured a vodka sold under the name Wodka Gorbatschow." "Why was the secretary general of the Communist Party running away from the revolution?" "It wasn't him, it was someone else." "So why did this other Gorbachev flee the revolution?" "Because he was very rich and egotistical and didn't want to share his fortune with others." "Why did he choose Berlin?" "I don't know."

The student from Bochum was named Jörg. For the past year he'd been studying Russian literature in Moscow. Now, on his return journey, he wanted to have a look at "East Berlin." Why did he say East Berlin and not simply Berlin? At this moment it occurred to me that this "Bochum" might perhaps be situated in the zone occupied by the Americans. My heart, which was already beating quite audibly on account of the vodka, began to beat even faster and louder. "Are your parents already asleep up in their hotel room?" he asked me. "They're at home in Saigon." "Did you come to Berlin all on your own?!" "Do I look so young? There are women my age who have children already." Jörg looked at me in surprise, finished his vodka without a word and ordered another glass. I regretted what I'd just said and added: "Of course, that's the exception. Women try to get married as late as possible and usually only give birth to a single child. This is our modern notion of population control, which I find quite sensible." But Jörg seemed utterly uninterested in Vietnamese politics; instead he was gazing attentively at the seam of my white blouse. The waiter who had not brought me a single potato brought us one vodka after the other. Perhaps all the potatoes had turned into vodka. In the First and Third Worlds, it was common political practice to use alcohol and other drugs to numb the population so that people wouldn't notice their hunger. Yet here I was in the Second World. Why was I getting only vodka and not potatoes?

Jörg started to talk about the Pergamon Museum. I wanted to ask if there really was a bird called Pergamon, but his tongue moved ever more slowly and clumsily. Unable to understand him, I began to get bored. "I'm going to bed," I told him. He seized my right arm with tong-like fingers and hastily whispered in my ear: "Tomorrow we're going to Bochum together." "Most certainly not," I replied. Jörg pressed his lips against my earlobe and asked: "Don't you want freedom?" His breath was a vodka ghost. "Why are you talking about freedom? What does freedom have to do with Bochum?" Suddenly electricity shook the air around us. The bass and the electric guitar filled the room with the sound of a gigantic construction site, and the prelude to "Katyusha" began. I saw Jörg's mouth opening and closing. He was no doubt saying something, but his words were immediately ground to dust by the electric sounds. I said that I couldn't hear a thing, but I couldn't even hear the words from my own mouth. We continued our vehement discussion without hearing each other. The large red cloth hanging above the stage displayed the Russian words "Peace to the World." The letters began to stand out more and more against the background until they dissolved in a blur. When the song was over, I could hear only the sound of my own heart pounding. I remembered that this was the first time in my life I'd ever been to a foreign country. And now a strange man from the enemy half of the world was filling my ears with incomprehensible words. To keep my heart from beating even faster and leaping out of my mouth, I picked up my glass and gulped down what remained of my vodka. Jörg said, his tongue reeling, "It's such a shame that a woman of your talents is living in the East." "I was invited to Berlin, not Bochum." It wasn't easy to argue against Bochum since I didn't know anything about this city. Perhaps it was possible to assert that Bochum lacked revolutionary, world-historical importance, or that it had never produced a famous writer who was known even in Vietnam. "Why don't you want to come with me?" Red spiderwebs stretched across Jörg's eyes. The musicians began to play again, this time sentimentally. "In my opinion, life has no meaning if I don't like the food." "You'll get used to it right away." "I don't speak German." "It won't take you long to learn." Since I didn't know what else to say, I simply cried out: "I want to go home! Home! Home!" This much I still remember. I heard the lead singer from the band raise his voice to sing: "*Rossia, Rossia, Rossia, my homeland!*" And the powerful waves of the melody swallowed up my consciousness.

•

When I woke up, I was lying on a rectangle of white sheet. Jörg stood at the foot of the bed, smiling. My body felt heavy and sank deeper into the softness of the mattress. On the wall was a poster of Sputnik. The window frames appeared oddly rectangular. Of course window frames in Vietnam are usually rectangular as well, but this was the first time I found their shape disturbing. When had I fainted? A day ago? A week? Or had it been even longer? The lost time was perceptible in my body only in the form of exhaustion. "Where are we now?" "In the West." I thought he meant West Berlin. So I said to him: "I've got to ride the streetcar to the East right away. I don't want to be late for the assembly." "You can't go to Berlin today. We're in Bochum."

When he said these words, a bottle of champagne that had been given a good shaking popped open in my head. In the distance, the noise of a siren erupted. Several seconds passed before I understood the siren was my own voice. When Jörg's face appeared in my field of vision again, I screamed in Russian: "I want to go home, home, home!" In a foreign language it sounded like a lie. Then I started crying because I was afraid of the silence. Crying almost made me forget why I was crying, and in order to reassure myself of the situation, I repeated: "I want to go home!" Jörg remained silent, his eyebrows drawn together. Then he said softly: "You can't go abroad from here. There isn't any airport in Bochum. And there's a reason why it's better for you to stay." "What reason?" "My child is in your belly. It would be smarter for us to start a happy family first and then go visit your parents together. You can't return home alone with this belly, not after you didn't even contribute to the assembly."

I got up without knowing what direction to go. My feet were cold. On the desk I saw a pair of sharp scissors. What did Jörg cut with such big scissors?

"What would you like to eat?" "Pho." "What?" "A certain kind of noodle." "What kind?" Since I was unable to explain in Russian that one must boil long thin rice noodles in water, add lime, raw bean sprouts, lemongrass, chili peppers, and the herb *ngò gai*, and then pour broth over the top, I summarized the cooking process: "Soup, noodles, and raw vegetables, mixed together." Jörg left the house while I fell back into bed hoping that sleep would undo everything that had happened.

When I woke up again, dinner was on the table, the food exactly as I had described except that the various ingredients were served separately. The noodles were thick and dull, smeared bloody with tomato sauce. Globules of fat floated on the surface of the soup, which tasted salty. There was also crumpled-up iceberg lettuce and hard tomatoes with mayonnaise. My uncle sometimes ate rice with mayonnaise. This was a Japanese product with a strange name: "Cupid Mayonnaise" or something like that. And indeed the image of the ancient god Cupid, who is said to have driven other gods and human beings into a state of infatuation, was depicted on the plastic tube. My father, who despised his brother, said to me: "All that illiterate cares about is acquiring foreign products and showing off." My uncle was not illiterate, but he was in the habit of saying that reading weakened male potency. "That isn't true, Uncle. Have your ears forgotten the voice of Ho Chi Minh? Did he not say to all the children of our land that reading and writing were the most important things to prepare one for life? He must have said this. I learned it at school." Unfortunately the President died three years before I was born, and so my own ear never experienced his voice.

I began to eat the lettuce with the white plastic fork. The taste of mayonnaise reminded me of the word pregnancy.

Jörg's bed was much too large in proportion to the room, which made me feel confined. I left the bedroom and went into the kitchen, where Jörg was producing a blubbering sound. "Would you like some coffee?" "No thank you. How did we get across the border?" "In my car." "Didn't the border police say anything?" A small, fat-bellied machine in one corner was spitting brown liquid into its own transparent belly. This liquid was supposed to be coffee even though it looked thin and meager. "You were disguised as the stuffing of the passenger seat. The policemen couldn't see you. Don't you know about TTT, Trabi Transport Technique? Are you sure you don't want any coffee?"

"No! I don't want any weak coffee!" If you wanted to offer me coffee, I thought, you would have to import Vietnamese coffee beans and then patiently roast them. You would have to roast them and roast them until they had a majestic black aroma.

Jörg said nothing, he turned his back to me and drank his coffee without milk or sugar. Surely some Western European company had deceived South American laborers and bought these coffee beans from them for a few coins. I secretly wished the spirits of the underage workers who had died on the coffee plantation would appear to Jörg in the night and torment him. When Jörg finished his coffee, he put on his leather jacket and left the house. The door made such a heavy, dull metallic sound when it shut that I thought it couldn't possibly be opened again for the next ten years.

Outside, the dusk was gathering. In the strangers' apartment across the way someone had turned on the light, though it wasn't possible to see into the room since the curtains with lace trim that reminded me of women's underwear blocked off the lower half of the windows. On the windowsill was a white porcelain statue of a fat, naked child. The child smiled diplomatically, sticking his penis out in my direction. The word "Belgium" was written on the little pedestal he stood on.

Usually I wasn't afraid of shadows. But when the shadow of a car swept across the bedroom wall, it sent a chill down my spine. When the shadow was gone, the uneven bits of wall that remained behind were more clearly visible than before. The wall resembled pubescent skin with countless tiny blisters. Squeezing them beneath my fingernails would release the smell of mayonnaise. The wall was as perfectly rectangular as the window and ceiling, but perhaps would feel slightly warm to the touch, like human skin.

I woke to my own screams, though I'd been neither sleeping nor dreaming. Three legs were growing out of my abdomen. Two of them were already familiar to me, but the third was muscular and hairy. When I screamed again, the third leg vanished. I remembered my uncle standing on a tall ladder once to repair the roof. It was a particularly hot summer day, and he was wearing shorts. Where in the world was Jörg?

A lamp by the bed resembled a giant mushroom. I hunted around for the switch, touching the shade and the stem as well, but nothing happened.

On the bed lay a saggy pillow. If I put my head on it, my head would sink deeper and deeper without stopping, it would sink through the mattress down to the floor, or even deeper—deeper and deeper, into the cellar, on and on until my head was buried in the earth.

Suddenly I was back on top again, or more precisely, I was on a stage, sitting on a cushion. Some three hundred young East German Party members sat in formation before me, listening with great concentration. Why did I have to sit alone on a cushion on the floor while everyone else had chairs? It must have been a cultural misunderstanding. In Japan or Iran, people might sit on the floor during a Party assembly, but not where I was from, and not in China either! But now it was our task to overcome these minor cultural differences and unite for the sake of peace on earth. I had been commissioned to speak about the violence of Capitalism. Unfortunately, I could not remember the contents of my speech because my cushion was distracting me. This cushion must have been a different manifestation of Jörg—for reasons unknown to me he'd been transformed into this pillow. He'd be unable to breathe if I sat on him with all my weight. So I tried to keep my hips in the air by contracting the muscles in my upper thighs. This position required a gymnastic exertion. At the same time I was trying not to press too hard, or else liquid micro-homunculi might get squeezed out of my vagina. What would the audience say if I gave birth to such creatures? "You speak well, but in reality you are nothing more than a treacherous housewife who desires foreign currencies and spits out children like interest rates!" It had already occurred to me that I might become the target of such reproaches. In Vietnam I was a model student, but no one here would believe that. People would immediately think I was voluntarily offering feminine charms as a commodity. Our neighbor,

Thailand, is constantly misunderstood and abused, and all of us suffer from these prejudices. Even the Japanese are partly responsible. Why did they export the word "geisha"? Perhaps they didn't have a choice, perhaps one hundred years ago they ran out of things to export. But we still pay the price today as potential geishas. "A capitalist country is always forced to export something, even if it is unprofitable and requires great sacrifices. The case of Japan most clearly demonstrates the contradictions inherent in capitalist economics, but soon other countries will be affected as well!" This is how, for the moment, I ended my speech. Self-praise is no virtue, but I was pleased to have ended my argument on such a strong note. No applause could be heard. Perhaps the audience was expecting me to say more about Vietnam. "In our country, many were sacrificed like laboratory rats to develop new weapons for the imperialist wars." A deathly silence reigned in the hall. The back of my neck was damp with cold sweat. The overpowering silence was unfortunate, as now the breathing of the pillow could be heard. In order to induce the audience to start laughing loudly, I tried to tell a joke: "By the way, according to the Chinese calendar I'm a rat. One of my teachers who speaks German recommended that I describe myself in Berlin as a mouse and not a rat, since the rat is widely despised in Germany. And so, esteemed comrades, let's say we were the *mice* in military experiments, not rats!" No one laughed. The hush was oppressive, and my breath hung heavy in my lungs.

The two young men who'd picked me up from the airport entered through the door at the back of the auditorium. They thrust their hips from side to side as they walked, like models at a fashion show, and turned around to display the name "Lee" on their butts. Lee jeans were so expensive that not even a whole month of my father's salary could have covered two legs. And of course at home we had many more legs than two to clothe. A classmate once told me the story of how the Lee company was founded. Once there was a Chinese man named Lee. He lived in a small village on the Yellow River and had such skillful fingers that he could even sew on buttons for ants. Out of boredom he emigrated to America and founded a company under his name.

The two men in jeans took the seats reserved for them in the first row. As I'd suspected, they were spies. They had already rolled up their sleeves and were waiting for a suitable moment to attack. When I began to speak about Doimoi politics, they climbed onto the stage and started stabbing my cushion with their knives. Blood spurted out, and I heard Jörg scream. The two spies explained to me in a brotherly tone: "He's a spy from Bochum. He wanted to rape you politically." Staring at the blood, I called Jörg's name longingly, as if he were my lover.

Someone was caressing my hair. Beside me lay Jörg. "What's the matter? Did you have a bad dream? Don't worry. No more bad things can happen here." He spoke sympathetically, like a brother consoling his much younger sister. Something similar had happened to me years before. Jörg's breath smelled of toothpaste with artificial lemon flavor. Then he covered my mouth with his so that my breath began to flow backward. The first time I ever ate duck tongue, I had a similar experience. My father's family came from the South. One of his sisters, who owned a restaurant in Saigon where she served, among other things, Chinese specialties, put a piece of duck tongue in my mouth and exhorted me, "Try it!" I was still young and didn't know whether or not I should bite into the duck tongue. Perhaps it was still alive. The tongue would begin to speak in two voices if I bit it in half; the taste would be as bitter as blood. If I tried to swallow the whole piece without chewing, I would be unable to breathe. And if I spat out the tongue, the grown-ups would laugh at me. What was I to do?

Jörg wasn't in the room. It was pitch black, and I couldn't hear the breath of any living creature. If I were to get up, leave the bed and wander around, I might never find the bed again—my lifeboat. I decided to shut my eyes and wait until the morning cast its rectangular, intact light into the room.

Every morning Jörg snapped shut his leather briefcase demonstratively and left for the university. When he came home late in the afternoon, he read Russian books with the help of a dictionary. After sundown he would order pizza and salad for us by telephone, sit with me for a moment, watch a few minutes of television, and then leave the house again. I was usually lying in bed by the time he returned, and would listen to the rustling of his shirt and trousers in the dark. I wasn't certain it was really Jörg. The one who was either Jörg or someone else would then crawl into bed. He smelled of old sofa, cigarettes, hair tonic, and carnations.

The first week, Jörg showed me department stores and restaurants, though I liked neither the heavy silverware on the white tablecloths nor the squeaky-clean panes of the shop windows. It was as if my tongue were paralyzed. Everything I ate tasted of fat and salt. The products in the department stores looked like collections of glittering trash. Every time Jörg spoke to me, the same question came out of my mouth: Why had he brought me here? Jörg took refuge in adjectives, saying to me: "We're going to a good department store, you'll see, a good one," "It's an inexpensive restaurant," or, "We'll go shopping at a nice shoe store."

A long, narrow pair of scissors was on the desk. On the blades, two angular little men could be seen, standing there hand in hand. Before a man whose name was probably Jörg climbed on top of my body at night, I held the scissors in readiness against my chest, blades closed and with the tip pointing to the sky. In the dark, the man couldn't see the scissors. He flung himself on top of me, and the scissors pierced his flesh. I could feel the blades piercing the space between his ribs. Perhaps their tips were already poking out of his back. His eyes swelled and popped. Then the heavy body fell beside me, sapped of its strength. It seemed as if there might be peace in the room for a while. Peace to the world: My work was completed. Suddenly it struck me that my hands felt sticky. Surprised, I realized that under conditions of very low light, human blood could look black.

A person's face looks strange when viewed from too close up. The eyes and eyebrows grow together, behind them a dark hollow opens up, the shape of the nose vanishes, the nostrils turn blacker, while the enamel surface of the teeth takes on a cannibalistic brightness.

The flesh of my buttocks was still stinging from Jörg's fingernails burning into my flesh. His heavy body, which I couldn't even push to the side a little, was crushing me. I stuck out my index finger and poked him in the eye. He gave a brief cry, jumped up, and ran into the bathroom, cursing. I followed him. He was examining his red eye in the mirror. I picked up the iron candlestick and slammed it into the back of his head. He sank slowly to his knees like an accordion being compressed, until finally he was flat on the floor. I blew into his ear to blow him up like a rubber doll. The moment he got up again, he kicked me in the chest. I fell backward, struck the back of my head against the wall and collapsed. Jörg grabbed me by the ankle, lifted it easily into the air and held me upside-down. Then he opened the lips of my vulva with his fingers and stuffed everything he could find inside: the toothbrush, the electric razor, the little bottle of eye drops, the comb. Only the nail scissors slipped from his hand. I grabbed them and stabbed his instep.

I soon became bored with sexual relations because it was always just the two of us and the scenery never changed. From the window I sometimes observed strangers leaving the building with serious expressions on their faces, hurrying off somewhere. "Don't you have any friends? Is there no one at all who takes an interest in you?" I asked Jörg, which made him look at me in surprise. The very next day he brought a man his age home with him. When I said to him in Russian that it was a pleasure to meet him, he looked embarrassed and replied in English that unfortunately he didn't speak Vietnamese. Jörg laughed and clapped him on the shoulder. Jörg told me that hardly anyone in this city spoke Russian. I was just as disappointed by this fact as when I'd heard there was no international airport. "This is Mark," Jörg re-introduced me to the man and began to drink cans of beer with him and chat.

Mark promised to bring his new girlfriend with him the next time he visited; she was originally from Moscow.

According to the explanations Jörg gave me later, Mark was very successful in his studies of economics but had no talent for languages. Although he'd once started to learn Russian, he couldn't even distinguish this language from others when he heard it spoken aloud. If a person looked Vietnamese, he would automatically hear Vietnamese. Faces looked different, but all foreign languages were the same to him in their incomprehensibility.

Mark's girlfriend was named "Anna," but she bore no resemblance to the Anna in my old Russian textbook. The new Anna didn't tell me in Russian how many brothers and sisters she had or where she was born. She didn't ask me in Russian how I was or what I would be doing next Sunday. Instead, she spoke German. I thought this Russian-less Anna should be called Anne instead of Anna. But what was I, who no longer spoke at all?

Jörg and I had a date with Mark and Anna at a pizzeria. Women and men in their early 20s were standing around. A few of them were waiting for their "fresh baked" pizza from the microwave, others were kissing or smoking. There was a slot machine with pictures of tomatoes in its windows.

Now and then Mark would give me a charming smile, while Anna never looked at me and remained immersed in conversation with Jörg. Coming from Anna's mouth, the German language sounded colorful and vivid. Listening to her I felt as if I were walking through hilly landscapes. The pizza tasted like old paper with a tomato flavor. The dark-red carbonated beverage tasted like sore-throat medicine. I would much rather have drunk fresh water with lime and sugar. A wave of sentimentality washed over me, perhaps because I was having my period. While we cut the pizza into little bits and ate them, I surrendered to a vision of Vietnamese spring rolls with fresh herbs, which made me salivate. Joylessly finishing my pizza, I still had nothing to say and sat there silently, my back hunched. Jörg must have felt sorry for me—he suddenly started to speak Russian. He asked Anna if she knew about the Trans-Siberian Railroad extension passing through Bochum. This railway line once provided a direct link between Moscow and Paris. Anna's face brightened: "Yes, I know. Don't the tracks run beside *Sieben Planeten*?" "There was a coal mine there," Mark added. "Do you know the American film in which a boy whose father is a poor miner sees the light from Sputnik in the sky one night and later becomes an astronaut?" "I've never seen an American film," I replied. Anna gave me a disgusted glance. "I like Tarkovsky," I added in protest. Anna laughed. Her face began to glow with amicability, and later she even bought me an ice cream.

Sieben Planeten, Seven Planets: these were the first two German words I consciously learned. When I thought of the planets in the cosmos, I was temporarily released from all my fears. This was a new discovery for me: Imagining an enormous distance without fear. So if I felt afraid, it must be due to things being too close.

Later I asked Jörg whether the train from Moscow to Paris really did once pass through Bochum. Jörg replied like a proud elementary school student eager to win praise from his teacher: "Yes, certainly. The train traveled from the Far East. It must have smelled of the Pacific seaweed that collects on the coast of Vladivostok, or like the stones of the Great Wall of China, the sand of the Mongolian desert or the salty waters of Lake Baikal. The train crossed the Urals to reach Moscow, then passed through Bochum on its way to Paris." "This means that we aren't living at the edge of the world after all, but rather along a major thoroughfare. From here you can take the train anywhere." Jörg's eyes clouded over. "What I don't know is if the train ever stopped here. I'll ask someone."

That night I couldn't sleep. Jörg was snoring. When I held the wings of his nose shut with two fingers, he quieted down. From a distance I could hear the faint grating sound of the drive axle, the clatter of the couplings, and a long, howling reverberation from the train tracks. Somewhere not far from my pillow a train was passing. Only insomniacs were aware of its existence.

I left the house and walked without direction or plan until I was tired. Then I retraced my steps, without having accomplished anything. "Sparrow" was the name of that small, brown, ordinary bird. When I stayed home, the same thoughts kept circling in my head. Can I really go to Saigon after the child is born? How much longer will the embryo remain in my belly? How old does the child have to be to fly? If my big sister or my mother were here, I could ask them all these things. My mother used to love teaching me about sexuality, as if she were determined to turn me into an utterly feminine dumpling. The human soul was spherical, she would insist, and even the body of a woman must be made of curves. I never listened to her and would interrupt or change the subject by quoting Confucius. He wrote, for example, that he had never encountered a person who preferred science to "colors." The Chinese ideogram for color can mean many different things. What Confucius surely meant here was sexual desire. "That's obvious," my mother would answer dismissively, "Who could be more interested in science than sexual intercourse?" If I had known my way around Confucius better, I would've told her many more things to make her fall silent. But I'd imported my knowledge only secondhand, or more precisely, secondmouth. An old teacher had started talking to me about Confucius during recess after he'd noticed my interest in his philosophy. I myself couldn't read Chinese characters. Surely it must be exciting to be able to write, say, the ideogram for "color," which supposedly resembles a squatting woman with a man on top of her. Such characters, I imagined, had to be far more exciting than my mother's sexual realism. "I think it's a shame I can't read Chinese." "Well, would you rather read Confucius and Mao than spruce up your appearance?" "You have something against China. Don't you realize how silly that is?" Confucius said one should not contradict one's parents. But what was I supposed to do if my foolish parents were against Confucius? Sometimes I imagined the heady odor of ancient Chinese books. It might have protected me from the smell of women that always filled our house like rotten mangos.

I wrote a letter to my family telling them that I had unexpectedly received a scholarship to study in Germany and therefore was planning to remain here a while longer. I intentionally wrote Germany and not Bochum so they wouldn't worry. Jörg observed me with a nervous expression when I asked him for stamps. To reassure him, I translated the letter aloud. He then tore it from my hand, put it in his leather bag and promised he would mail it for me.

One month went by without my hearing anything from my family. Jörg didn't have a calendar on his wall, but since I was having my period again, I knew that approximately one month must have passed. Why didn't my family write to me? Had they forgotten me like an aborted child? Was my family under surveillance and thus unable to write back? Back in the 70s, there were parents who sent their talented children into exile alone because they thought their individual development more important than keeping the family together. But wasn't the notion of exile outdated? In my class at school there was a girl who'd just returned with her family from Switzerland.

Between the room's four walls I was plagued with anxieties. Out on the street, however, I no longer felt I was cut off from the past. I tried to get away from the idea that there were separate places called "here" and "there." Despite the distance between them, "here" and "there" had to be connected. The Berlin Wall was said to be more difficult to break through than the Great Wall of China, but on the map of the world in Jörg's room I discovered an unbroken line that reached from Vladivostok to Lisbon. Bochum wasn't on the map. There was no desert in the Western part of Europe. The names of so many different cities were represented that the lines of letters touched. How strange it was to think that the existence of these cities whose names I didn't know wasn't somehow having an effect on my day-to-day life.

There were a few warm days, but the windows of the neighborhood houses remained closed. In front of the windows grew well-formed flowers that resembled plastic flowers. Hardly anyone planted vegetables in their gardens. Apparently they didn't need any. Even Jörg hardly ate any vegetables except tomatoes.

My steps grew swifter with each passing day, my eyes

wanted to take in more and more. If the day before I walked as far as the house with the little wreath of fir twigs, today I would walk to the house with the grinning plastic dolls. These dolls were wrinkled old men wearing red nightcaps and felt boots. Since I had to begin at the same starting point every day, I walked faster and faster to go even farther. It stayed light out later and later, and between five and nine o'clock time stood still. I didn't own a watch. When the sun was still shining innocently bright, it might already be nine in the evening. I found this deceptive brightness unsettling, and the way back always seemed to take me much longer. The few shops on Jörg's street closed punctually at six o'clock. After six there was no one anywhere on the streets although the sun was still shining. The sun illuminated only me, an unimportant character playing a non-speaking role in a theater with no audience.

Once I returned home so late that Jörg was already back from his pub crawl. "Where have you been?" Jörg spoke German to me more and more often. I was doing my best not to learn this language. I was afraid it might fetter me to this place forever. I didn't need to understand German either. The situation and Jörg's face showed me clearly what he meant. He also had no intention of teaching me. Jörg seemed to be waiting for me to become a part of his familiar surroundings of my own accord, just as a new, over-starched shirt eventually becomes as supple as a second skin.

Our shared life made us more and more mute. Jörg no longer told any stories, and I didn't know what to talk about. His wishes were not difficult to discern. He always wanted to eat exactly the same thing. When he was tired from studying, he wanted to rest. When he wasn't watching TV, it might occur to him to have sex. Here, too, he never thought to modify the fixed scenario by means of words. First there were cold lips, then a hot tongue. My breasts became dough to be kneaded, and then I was overwhelmed by a certain sensation as if I were about to pee. At the same time I watched with detachment as Jörg's head moved up and down. Now and then he would turn my body over as if frying a fish. I felt ashamed to turn my back to him. Since I couldn't see him, he seemed too naked to me. It was just the same with my face. I didn't like it when he gazed at my face too long. "You don't have to be ashamed, other people do exactly the same thing. You see it in movies," he explained to me.

The idea of a railway line stretching all the way from Paris through Bochum to Moscow never left my head. One day, immediately upon awakening, the question leapt out of my mouth without forethought: "Did you ever ask anyone about the train tracks near *Sieben Planeten*?" Jörg had one leg in his pants, the other was still hovering in the air. "Not yet. But you can go there yourself if it interests

Yoko Tawada

you so much." Jörg gave me directions. It didn't seem to be any longer a trip than my daily walks, just in a different direction. "My mother walked there herself when she was visiting. Otherwise she was bored staying with me. She said the fields of rapeseed were gorgeous." I was surprised that Jörg had a mother. Why had she been bored staying with him? Was it boring to have a son? Why didn't Jörg want to introduce me if we were to marry soon?

I followed Jörg's instructions and found a street called "Sieben Planeten." Three little boys were playing with a toy tractor. It was rare to see children playing on the street. There were probably dangerous kidnappers in the region. At the end of the street, a wide vista suddenly opened up, and I was received by the light of the rapeseed fields. The entire surface of the earth was yellow to the horizon. Why did they need so much vegetable oil? There were so few vegetables in this city. Did they like cooking just a few vegetables with lots of oil, or did the oil get used for military purposes? A narrow path led through the middle of the field. To the left and right stood the rapeseed plants that were only a tiny bit shorter than I was. Does a politician have a similar feeling when he walks through the crowd that is receiving him? It seemed I was being welcomed. "Our comrade has come from far away to share her knowledge with us. Let us greet her with applause!" An applause of rapeseed blossoms. I was a model student and always arrived on time for the assembly of young Party members. At the right edge of the field, the inviting shade of a dark green forest beckoned. The path curved toward the forest.

The rapeseed field was tugging at my hair with invisible hands. The plants wanted me to stay with them. But a different force was propelling me forward, in the direction of a road where the houses appeared to have been not so much constructed as arrayed. There was not a living creature anywhere to be seen: the windows were clean and shiny, the walls of the buildings flawlessly smooth. My shoes were making a strange hollow sound, as if I were walking through a tunnel in high heels. There must have been large hollow spaces beneath my feet. No wonder—for this country, too, had experienced wars. Or had miners worked beneath this bit of road? The houses thrust me away with innocent faces. An old man came out of one of the houses to pluck invisible weeds among his tulips. He turned his turtle shell on me. I kept walking.

At the end of the street, a small forest began. The shadows of the oak trees suddenly appeared more familiar to me than the human habitations. Would it perhaps be better for me to live in a forest than in a city? No, a large cross said to me. Its limbs were white with red tips. At first I couldn't see the grass-covered railway tracks on the far side of the cross. The rails were rusty, perhaps many years had passed since they'd last been used, perhaps no one had even looked at them in all this time. The tracks disappeared to the left in the shade of trees, to the right in the sunny no-man's-land.

These train tracks summoned up a secret link tying together the past months and days that hadn't vanished and gone astray. It excited me to think that the tracks I saw before me continued all the way to Moscow. A cousin of mine was studying in Moscow. I didn't know his address, but I would surely be able to find him right away since people there would be able to understand me. My cousin would put me on a direct train to Peking. In Peking I would buy a ticket to Hanoi. There might be complications, but compared to my present situation, those other problems would be tiny peas. From Hanoi it would take only another two days to reach Saigon, and surely nothing else bad could happen to me on this stretch of the journey. If only I could get to Moscow!

I wanted to wait for a train to board, but there was no train station. I returned several times on other days and walked along the tracks in both directions. I found no trace of any station present or past. Nor did I ever see a train pass by. Only on sleepless nights when I lay in bed, my eyelashes on fire, could I hear the sound of a train far off in the distance.

Jörg was sitting at the kitchen table scowling, his chin propped in both hands. "What happened?" This was a question I could now ask fluently in German. I loved the word for "happened," *passiert*. It gave me the feeling that everything that happened to a person would soon pass over. Nothing was forever. The only thing I still possessed from my past life was my passport, which I always kept in my breast pocket. "I flunked the exam," Jörg said. Like a big sister, I placed my hand on his head and said: "No problem. Try again!" He took my hand and held it before his mouth like a microphone. "I'm not made for studying. My father isn't going to send me any more money. This was my last chance. I don't want to stay at the university. Why don't the two of us start working together. We can sell cars in the East Bloc." I nodded, since it made no difference to me whether he was a student or held a job. I was just surprised to learn he had a father. "What does your father do?" "He works in an office." "Aren't we going to visit your parents?" "No, it's out of the question." Jörg got up and put his wallet in his pants pocket. "Where are you going?" "I just want to have a beer, then I'll be back."

An hour went by, and then another, but Jörg did not return. The light brown leather shoes he never wore were sitting in one corner of the room. Out of boredom I started pushing them back and forth with my feet like a soccer player in a slow-motion replay. The second hand of the wall clock advanced with a tremble. I imagined breaking off the hand. Then I decided to go out for a walk. As soon as I reached the end of the street, inky clouds began to flood the sky.

I regretted setting off in this weather and spoke the words "Sieben Planeten" aloud, then nothing frightened me anymore. I could smell the approaching rain.

Another woman was already standing in my favorite spot by the rusty tracks. Her long coat had a high collar that resembled the gills of a tropical fish. On her head she wore ornaments that looked somehow extraterrestrial. Perhaps she was a singer who'd fled from the stage of an opera with futuristic sets. What could be the reason for her having hurried here without removing her makeup and changing clothes? She was older than I was, and had something extraordinary about her. Her presence even seemed to be changing the consistency of the air around her. The clear form of her lips held her flesh together like overripe fruit, and the two ends sometimes dipped down slightly, as if they were remembering a bitter taste. The woman's spine described a straight line of justice not dependent on any existing law. Each time I blinked, her body dissolved for two seconds into colorful micro-grains.

The darkness around us thickened. The woman gave me a dutiful nod, as if the two of us had an understanding. My heart began to pound violently. It was up to me to take action. Today was the chosen day. I had a vague memory of our having arrived at our agreement in a dream, though the specific terms of the agreement were unknown to me. Suddenly the woman lay down on the tracks and pressed her face to one of the ties. I ran to her, took her by the shoulder and tried to roll her over, but she was as immovable as the spire of a temple whose root is buried in the earth. I thought I heard the sound of a train approaching from a distance—this was impossible though. These tracks had known nothing but rust and weeds for years, certainly no wheels. Then I heard it once more, the sound of an approaching train. Or was it just a streetcar heading into the city center? Or was it the drone of a refrigerator that had been implanted in the depths of my eardrums during my days of loneliness? I wanted to tell the woman to get up, but I couldn't think of any words. The old words had left my skull, I needed new words to be able to speak to her. But what were new words? The heavy iron wheels continued to turn, coming closer and closer. I glanced about helplessly. Somewhere there had to be an alarm system. In a bush I saw something red—a box with a painted lightning bolt. A lever was growing crookedly out of the box like the tail of a dragon. It wouldn't budge. I pressed the lever down with the whole weight of my body, my legs dangling in the air, and then crashed down with the lever. The frozen silence gave way to a siren. Innumerable tiny red blinking lights set in a line at regular intervals into the distance began flashing on and off.

I hid behind a bush, and heard the train brake with an ear-rending whinny. A monstrous shadow stopped, eclipsing my field of vision. A white flower in a bush floated before my nose. For some reason the flower bothered me although it was giving off an enchanting fragrance. A pair of conductors jumped off the train and gathered about the prone woman. Arguing voices and confused footsteps circled in my head while my heart beat even louder. I wasn't afraid of being arrested. Perhaps they'd claim I had pushed the woman onto the tracks or had stopped the train unnecessarily. None of this would have disconcerted me. There was a question I found far more pressing, but I was afraid to translate it into a language. If I formulated the question, I would first have to give an answer and then take action. To Moscow, to Moscow, to Moscow. If I got on this train, I could ride to Moscow and from there find my way home. I crept through the bushes that ran alongside the train and reached its center. One side of a double folding door was still open from where a conductor had leapt out. I slipped into the train and walked down the deserted corridor. All the compartment doors were locked except for one at the end. White light seeped through a crack in the door. I opened the door carefully and saw a woman my age who looked like me. She immediately spoke a language that ambushed me and swallowed me up. The meaning of her sentences reached my brain cells at once: The woman had reserved a women-only compartment for two persons and had been horrified when no one else joined her. She hated to be alone in a closed-off little space—her relatives had already experienced more than enough of this. I immediately replied that I was in the exact same situation. With clots of tears in my throat I asked if I might spend the night in her compartment. She immediately gave an energetic nod as the siren of an ambulance wailed in the distance.

My countrywoman was named Ai Van, but unfortunately I couldn't refer to her as a comrade, for she had emigrated to France with her family when she was still a little girl. She had attended the Lycée Saint-Catherine in Paris, married a Frenchman, and was now pursuing a degree in film studies. As we spoke, the train began to move again.

This was the first time I'd ever spoken with an emigrant who was still living abroad. Before, I assumed all emigrants were more or less rich, fat, and egotistic with shoe and furniture fetishes. I thought you could recognize them at once by the cold gaze with which they judged their fellow men according to their clothes. I couldn't make any such claims with regard to Ai Van. I might have been talking to one of my girlfriends. I told her I'd married a German tourist I'd met in Saigon and now was living in Germany. "At the moment, though," I added, "I'm traveling through Europe alone to figure out what I want to study." "Where are you planning to stay in Paris?" Ai Van asked. It took me a little while to grasp the meaning of her question. I almost started screaming, "Isn't this train going to Moscow?!" In the faint hope of having misunderstood, I asked her when we were arriving in Paris. "Early tomorrow morning, I think," she replied gaily.

Everything went black before my eyes. The train grated

to a higher speed to aggrieve me. Moscow was drawing farther and farther away behind the invisible horizon. Ai Van's lips effervesced with the luxuriantly ornate names of Parisian buildings that didn't reach my ear. I already knew that Paris was a famous city. And the French Revolution certainly wasn't bad either—it was a revolution, after all. But I didn't know what I was going to do in Paris, which felt hopelessly far away.

My uncle once bragged that he might be offered the chance to take a business trip to Paris. My father replied with contempt that it was ludicrous when a person from a poor family of peasants who had recently acquired a decent standard of living only thanks to the revolution suddenly developed a longing for Paris.

Unlike my father, who despised his brother, my mother and her sister got along very well. My aunt once told me that as a young girl she and a friend had undertaken a secret expedition into the ruins of a rubber plantation. Her ancestors had owned this land. Beneath a large spiderweb stretched over a sofa like an umbrella, she sat down into the abandoned sofa from which the moldy dampness of the century was rising. My aunt and her friend discovered a trunk beside the sofa. Inside they found the dingy funnel of a gramophone and a few mold-covered books. My aunt flipped through them, took a single book—Balzac's *Seraphita*—home with her and tried to read a few passages here and there or rather guess at them. "Our country used to be part of France," my aunt told me when I was still quite small. I am supposed to have replied: "Then Paris was part of our country! How lovely!" My aunt laughed. This memory made me feel calmer.

When Ai Van learned that I scarcely had any money with me, she immediately pressed a few large bills into my hand without hesitation. Since I asked whether she knew of an inexpensive hotel, she offered to arrange for me to spend the night with her older sister. She couldn't bring me home with her as her younger sister was visiting. She wrote down a few addresses and telephone numbers for me.

Chapter Two

Zig zig

Numberless chimneys stuck out from the tile rooftops. Some of them were short and fat, others looked emaciated. I took one of the broad streets that began at the Gare du Nord and walked straight ahead without looking around so that anyone watching me would think I knew where I was going. Only the five-armed intersections made me uncertain. Here I could no longer say what "straight ahead" meant.

The sky's curtain was slowly being closed, and the wavy

pattern of the cobblestones darkened. Who had taken so much time to arrange these stones so precisely? How could they fit so neatly together? At the point where the pattern of waves gave way to a pattern of snake scales, it began to rain. I stopped in my tracks and looked back: the cobblestones had vanished, replaced by a dull asphalt street. I walked on. High-heeled footsteps approached from behind and overtook me. I saw nothing of the woman's face, only her tense back. Several others overtook me as well: a man who was pulling up the collar of his summer coat and walking bolt upright as if he might otherwise lose his head; an older woman who showed me her lonely-looking back— perhaps she'd just lost her poodle.

The dark, wet window frames made me think of rings beneath weary eyes. I didn't have the courage to show someone the slip of paper and ask directions. People flitted past, hurrying toward their unknown destinations.

A shop window filled with old miniatures depicting dogs attracted my attention. I pressed my nose up against the glass to get a better look at the miniatures and etchings. I'd never seen many of the breeds before, yet I realized for the first time in my life that I loved dogs. If I were a dog, I would immediately feel safe in any city.

The wet streets shone black as the snout of a healthy dog. Would the night eventually just swallow me up? I kept walking. The bright neon advertisements of the restaurants blurred together in the moist air.

Randomly turning into an alleyway, I found a shop whose plate-glass window displayed pink, light blue, and yellow umbrellas beneath glaring lights. Behind the counter, two saleswomen were arguing. One was much older than the other. Perhaps she was the other one's mother. There was a period when my older sister, too, argued with my mother on a daily basis. My mother didn't like my sister's lover. The argument reached its climax when my mother learned that my sister was pregnant. But then the argumentative phase gradually ended. When you get a high fever, your cold will soon be over—these were the words of wisdom my sister shared with me.

In another alleyway, two women stood wearing net-like stockings that reminded me of mosquito netting. One woman, whose dress was brown, had golden hair, while the other, who had chestnut brown hair, wore a golden chain. Both of them were attentively observing the passersby on the boulevard and didn't even notice I was standing in front of them. Soon a man turned off the boulevard and approached the women with a wobbly gait. This rather fat man, who had drawn his cap down until it all but covered his eyes, pulled some money out of his breast pocket and shook the bills before the nose of the chestnut-haired woman. To my surprise, she smiled at him, took his arm and led him into the darker part of the alley. I followed them and watched them go up the stairs of an old two-story building. Soon the light went on in one of the rooms. Apparently, the woman was renting rooms for the night. I had a few banknotes as well. Ai Van said I could easily live on this money for several days. Therefore it seemed excessive for this woman to be asking so much money for a room in this run-down building. My teacher always told us that it was a basic human right to be able to sleep beneath a roof and between four walls. Earning money by renting rooms, he said, was one of Capitalism's most grievous transgressions. If this was how people here lived though, I certainly wouldn't succeed in reeducating them overnight. It was already too late to look for the apartment of Ai Van's sister. Because of the mosquitoes I definitely didn't want to sleep outdoors. Here one could apparently get a room using sign language. I went back to the spot where the blond woman was still standing. She was so good-looking she ought to have been in the movies. Maybe she hated cameras, just like me. And who can say which is a better profession? I took out my banknotes and shook them before the nose of this woman, who was at least ten centimeters taller than me. She opened her large eyes even wider and batted her elegant, curved eyelashes. Although I hadn't done anything different than the man before me, the woman was so surprised she nearly froze. Impatiently I grabbed her by her bare upper arm, making her flinch and take a step back. I pointed in the direction of the old building where the other woman had disappeared with the man, and nodded at her, smiling.

She glanced quickly at my banknotes and assumed a pensive expression. Then she searched for something between my eyes and my mouth. She appeared to find whatever it was she was looking for as her frozen face relaxed a little. I took her by the hand and pulled her toward the entrance of the building.

A large oval mirror hung in the room. The mirror seemed to show me precisely what the woman, too, saw when she looked at me: a shy, scrawny girl. Only her eyes gleamed as if caught in a high fever, and her lips burned apple-red. Was this really me? In high school I was one of the girls who made a sturdy, mature impression. No one ever told me I was thin or looked childish. The mirror also showed the woman standing behind me. A dramatic curve descended from the back of her neck over her breasts and hips down to her thighs. A masterful brushstroke. When I turned to face her, she no longer resembled a two-dimensional work of art but rather was living matter heavy with flesh. She asked me something. I recognized the word "Papa." Perhaps she thought I was looking for somewhere to stay together with my father. I said in English, "Only for me." I always claimed not to know any English. But if I were to drum up every English word I knew, perhaps I could actually speak a little English. Was the woman afraid that without my father I wouldn't be able to pay for the room? I pressed my banknotes, which had grown somewhat moist with my sweat, into her hand. Then I had to squeeze her hand shut, because the woman was just staring at me and ignoring the money. Apparently there was something wrong with my face.

The woman sat down on the bed, and I sat down beside her. She seemed to be waiting for something. I tried to think what else one should do when renting a room. I couldn't think of anything. Perhaps she was just lonely. A bit of fuzz clung to her hair above the ear. I reached out my finger to remove it. The woman flinched as if she were afraid of me. What about my body could be so intimidating? Even if we were to quarrel and come to blows, she would be the victor. And above all: What would we quarrel about?

I remembered my great aunt who had died two years before. During the last months of her life she was afraid of things no one else could see. When I asked her what frightened her, she would say: "A soldier without legs came to see me" or "The bones buried beneath the kitchen sob at night." Once she poured cold water on herself and said her dress was on fire. She also told me that in the forest there was a charred tree stump from which headless children were born. The word "imagination" meant nothing to her, and a different word, "hallucination," was something she'd never heard. When I embraced her and stroked her cheek, her flesh would relax. She would then repeat "Thank you, thank you, thank you" and grow a little calmer.

This woman, too, young as she was, probably suffered from hallucinations like my great aunt. Out of pity I placed my arm around her neck and drew her to me. At first she tried with hesitant fingers to push my belly gently away from her. Then her fingers groped for my spine and read Braille. She asked me something I didn't understand. Maybe the meaning of the question was unimportant anyway. I couldn't comfort my great aunt with words either. Instead, one had to say yes to every question and calmly pet her. I nodded to the woman and stroked her cheek. For some reason I couldn't fathom, she pulled down the zipper of her dress, slipped out of this shell, and opened the hooks of her undergarments. Then she took my hand and pressed the tips of my fingers against her nipple, which felt like the toe of a cat. There was a tiny fissure at its center. Perhaps this fissure was where the mother's milk came out. I couldn't remember whether I too had a fissure like this. The woman seemed to have read my thoughts in my face. She unbuttoned my blouse with trembling fingers. My skin looked flat, inexpressive, shut off. Once her fingers began speaking to it, though, my skin began to open up, not just my nipples, but my whole body.

Suddenly I felt the inner wall of my stomach burning with hunger. I thought of the red of prawns shimmering through moist rice paper, or the white of steamed fish one carefully unwraps from a bamboo leaf. The woman asked me a question. As an answer, I placed my hand on my belly. The woman nodded without giving the impression she was about to get me some food. Instead, she stuck her fingers under my belly. At the same time I saw her lips in close-up, her wet teeth gleaming between them. From her mouth drifted a smell like lemongrass, making me dizzy. I lay down on my back, and the woman's skin blocked my vision. The white, warm skin melted on my tongue, but I didn't bite any off. I was in a round space, perhaps within a sphere. There was one fixed point on the inner wall of this sphere: the place where my temple touched hers. Both were as hard as stone, thoughtful, not melting together, waiting for something new. I was dreaming of peas. The peas were as hard as stone before they grew astonishingly soft in a pot of boiling water. I dreamt of oysters with lemon juice, eating them with a sobbing sound, my fingers taking on their fragrance.

I heard someone hurriedly unlocking the door from outside. The woman leapt up; in the doorway stood a man whose well-groomed brown hair hung down like the ears of a dachshund. The woman quickly covered us with the wool blanket while arguing hot-headedly with the man. Then she wrapped the sheet around her, got up and chased him out the door after hurling a few more explosive words in his face. From the floor I retrieved my neck pouch, which contained the money and my passport, and got dressed, while the woman, who had gotten dressed in two seconds, waited for me impatiently. Then she grabbed me by the wrist, ran out of the room and hurried down the steps. We rushed down the alley in the opposite direction to the boulevard. This was a network of dark but pleasant-smelling alleys. Eventually we arrived at the entrance to a building that looked charred. The woman didn't even have to hunt around for a light switch as her toes could clearly see the steps that led down to a basement. In the basement room the light switch was broken, but through the barred window one could see a little light reflecting off the cobblestones. Between the stacks of cardboard boxes with writing on them stood an animal with horns and a rusty bicycle. The woman sat me down on a box and pointed to the numerals eight and two on her watch. Then she left.

An old floor lamp exactly my height stood beside me. The lamp had a cable that vanished in a dark corner—a good place for an overlooked electrical outlet, but what good was an outlet for a lamp with no bulb? A deformed leather handbag at the base of the lamp was cracked and hard. Opening its metal navel wasn't easy. I held the bag upside-down. A crumpled, dried-up handkerchief fell out followed by lipstick, a ballpoint pen, and a flyer advertising a movie. The title of the film was *Zig zig*, and the date was already ten years in the past. This was the first time I saw your name. And this was the one film I was never able to see, even later. A long time passed before I understood that it wasn't necessarily important whether or not one has actually seen a film.

•

The woman was called Marie. She left the basement every evening and returned around two in the morning. When I sat alone in the basement, I felt like a hostage abducted by terrorists. The worst thing about these terrorists was that in reality they weren't making any demands and thus would never release me. Of course I wasn't locked up—I had unlimited freedom and could leave the basement if I wished.

Marie was not an abductor, she was my protector. She protected me by ignoring me. She acted as if she were unable to see me, or as if I were a wildflower that just happened to be growing in her garden. If only I'd been able to exchange just a few words with her. I couldn't understand her language, and she even seemed to be withholding it from me. When she returned from work, she would install herself in her favorite corner like a work of art for the world to see but was nonetheless unapproachable. I wouldn't have felt so useless if she had, for example, forced me to join her in her nocturnal perambulations. Or she could have threatened me with her knife and forced me to sell pears. Indeed, she possessed a double-edged knife, but she only used it to peel apples. I missed the sense of being bound to other people. Of course it wasn't right to offer up one's body—a gift from our ancestors—as goods for sale. And in any case the desire to provide a service as a way of earning money was a capitalist malaise. I remained behind in the basement, isolated and useless. If I'd had a child of my own, I'd at least have had a task. Perhaps this was the reason other people produced children. The child in my uterus had at some point vanished into thin air. Or the child existed from the very beginning merely as Jörg's phantom pregnancy.

During the day I walked around the city so as not to have to sit behind bars. The streets drove me on without a goal from one corner to the next, no armchair waited to receive my weary limbs. Be still, I said to the pavement beneath my feet, but it kept flowing on and on like a conveyor belt, and I was the automobile tire. I remembered the shoes called Ho-Chi-Minh sandals that were made from old tires. If I were to wear them here, they would be seen as a symbol not of frugality but of a ceaselessly increasing velocity.

Sometimes I saw policemen on the street. What would happen if I were to describe my situation to them and ask for help? "I let down the East Berliners who were expecting me to give a speech. I illegally crossed the border between East and West. A woman played the role of a would-be suicide to stop a train for me. From there, I traveled to Paris without a ticket. I borrowed money from a Vietnamese woman and never went to see her. I am living in a basement without paying rent. Yesterday I stole a rose from a flower vendor." If I were to tell my story freely, the policemen wouldn't help me, they'd arrest me. Candor is incompatible with freedom. Is a person any more able to find his way home from inside a prison? What would my relatives and above all my teachers and friends have to say about this? They would no doubt start collecting money right away so that my parents could come visit me in Paris. But what a shame it would be if their first trip to Paris was to see a jailbird. Besides, they would be utterly unable to help me here. In Saigon my father knew influential politicians—connections of no use to us in Paris. When I was younger, I never needed to keep any secrets. As long as I was honest, industrious, and modest, loved my friends, teachers, and family, nothing bad could happen to me. This security was now long gone. I had become a criminal without ever having had any intention of doing wrong, and without having so much as killed a bug. Someone once told me that in Paris one could place international phone calls even from a normal telephone booth. Was there also a direct line to the realm of the dead? I would have liked to call Confucius and Ho Chi Minh and ask them what to do.

If a policeman thought me suspicious, he might stop me and ask to see my passport. I always carried my passport with me, but I had no visa for France. Fortunately my Asian features did not make me conspicuous. This city was full of Asian-looking women. Most of them were in the habit of glancing into shop windows to check the quality and prices of handbags and dresses for sale. Sometimes, to my surprise, I caught a glimpse of my own mirror image, which always horrified me. You could tell from my body language that I had no intention of buying anything in the display window. Whenever a saleswoman looked at me through the glass door, trying to figure out what brand name might be of interest to me, I would hurry away. In my eyes, these brand names were simply crooked letters, pictograms whose meaning I could not discover. Anyone could see at a glance that I had no right to be here.

To escape the agitation of the streets, I sought refuge in movie theaters. One could linger here for hours for little money. In the dark there was no danger of being observed by a policeman. My first film was Polanski's *Repulsion*. On the poster for this film I discovered the name of the actress printed on the old flyer for *Zig zig*. This was why I could walk right up to the ticket window and courageously pronounce the film's title. *Repulsion* had been made twenty years before, and so my very first time seeing you was at a temporal remove.

The movie theater was even darker than the basement, though there was something reassuring about the space. On the screen strangers played out their lives for me to see. I couldn't imagine myself as a character living in Paris. For the first time, however, I could truly picture my own body in various positions. For instance, the first time I lay in bed in Bochum staring at the walls. I learned this from the bedroom scenes in *Repulsion*. It wasn't just me lying in bed, it was you.

Marie usually returned to the basement much later than I did. When I came back from the theater, I would rewind an invisible roll of film inside my head to watch the movie again from the beginning. My mental cinema boomed with a dull percussive sound. The characters fell silent. I saw the protagonist hurrying somewhere with long strides. Her fingers kept trying to remove something invisible from the wing of her nose. A skinned rabbit was stuffed in her handbag. Behind her armoire, a crack opened in the wall. A strange construction site in the middle of the busy street might have been a pedestrian island. An old neighbor woman wearing so many layers of clothing she appeared spherical stood at the door of the building with a hat and a dog. Three street musicians the size of children were playing accordion, clarinet, and drum. As they played, they slowly walked backward.

When I heard Marie's footsteps, all the images in my head vanished and I would greet her at the basement door. She would turn her face away from me as if in embarrassment, murmuring a few words I couldn't understand. Once I placed a delicate-scented rose I'd stolen in the city in the place where she slept. Marie ignored both me and the rose, her strong perfume stinging my nostrils like the scent of lilies in sickrooms that irritate the patients' mucous membranes and cause nightmares. A perfume war between the lily and the rose. Marie hid behind the scent of the lily. Since the night of the misunderstanding we hadn't touched

Yoko Tawada

each other. I felt that Marie was trying to keep me at a distance from her profession and had nothing else to offer me.

One day Marie came home with a book which she pressed into my hand while saying a few words in an encouraging tone of voice. The book was yellow with a large black-and-white photograph on the cover. At first I didn't recognize the woman in the picture. The word *Ecran* was printed in round letters on the cover next to two mysterious numbers: "78" and "73." Had Marie bought the book from a peddler on the street, or had a customer given it to her? I was surprised to discover a scene from *Repulsion* in the book: the main character, Carol, in the process of writing something on the surface of a mirror.

I remembered a situation I'd almost forgotten. I was standing outside, leaning against the cinema's wall as if drunk when Marie walked by and looked at me questioningly. I pointed to the poster I was leaning against. With the seriousness of a child learning to read, Marie read aloud each of the names on the poster: director, actors, actresses. When she read your name, I nodded.

At the time I didn't know that *Ecran* was a magazine and not a book. The books I'd read as a schoolgirl had been similarly bound and were as thin as this journal. *Ecran* became my first language textbook. All night long, my hot temples refused to sleep. With the help of this book, I would learn the language, then I'd study philosophy at the university, join the Party and rise among its ranks. Eventually the Party would come to power and I would become a leader. I would give an apartment to every person who lived in a basement, and I too would move into such an apartment, perhaps together with Marie. We would look out our big window at a big walnut tree in which spirits liked to linger. Fresh water free of bacteria would flow out of the faucets at any time of the day. The water might smell a little like a swimming pool, but even the odor of the chlorine would seem pleasant to me as it would remind me more of my summer vacations as a child than of a hospital. In the mornings, Marie would use the subway pass distributed free of charge at the factory to ride comfortably to work, where she would don a blue uniform that she didn't have to wash herself but could simply drop off at the laundry department after work. In the evenings she would always come home on time since working overtime was illegal. Without a care in the world, she would hop in the bathtub. Of course, it would be much more fun to bathe in a large bathhouse with all our friends. But it would be fine with just the two of us as well. We would no longer eat with plastic forks and knives from plastic plates held on our laps, but instead would sit at a table and use bamboo flatware. The rats and mice that tormented us in the basement would not be found in our new apartment. They would willingly go live in the forest. Then again, I wasn't quite sure whether they did in fact come from forests or had always lived in basements. If the latter, public basements would be created for the rodents so they wouldn't have to live out in the wild.

When the sunlight shone past the window bars the next morning, I caught the glimmering light in the open book in my hands. Between pages eleven and twenty-five were sixteen photos of you: four close-ups of your face, and twelve scenes from various movies. This was the day I consciously began addressing you in the second person, although I didn't know you yet and you remained utterly unaware of my existence.

Out of your many faces I constructed a single face, and this one face differed from all the others I saw in the city. Other women's eyes could never quite capture my gaze; their noses appeared to have been artificially constructed, their mouths randomly affixed. Incidentally, I always forgot to include myself when I thought of these "other women." My person vanished in the darkness of the movie theater, and all that remained was my burning retinas reflecting the screen. There was no longer any woman whose name was "I." As far as I was concerned, the only woman in the world was you, and so I did not exist.

Two shop windows, a mirror, a bicycle.
A piano, a bed, a wheelchair.
A doll, two wine glasses, an empty sky.

A dining table, wind, a pistol.

Three scenes were reproduced on each page as in a comic book, but without any sort of plot connecting them for these scenes were taken from different films. Most of them I hadn't seen.

Page fifteen. Top: you are standing in front of a shop window with a woman who is showing off her healthy teeth. Center: you are writing on a mirror in an invisible script that probably isn't simple mirror-writing any longer for the script has been reversed three times now—first in the mirror, then in the film, then in the photograph. Bottom: you are sitting on a bicycle, about to ride off. An old man is standing beside you, trying to hold you back. In the background one sees a shabby courtyard. Your lush, luminous hair is fluttering in the imaginary wind as if you are already pedaling through the fields.

Page eighteen. Top: you and a second woman your age who bears a magical resemblance to you are standing side by side in front of a piano. Both of you are positioned with your hips pointing back behind you, but your faces are turned stalwartly ahead. Perhaps this is part of a dance step that has been fixed in place in the photograph. Both of you are wearing large summer hats. On the piano one sees a large sheet of music and a black metronome. It isn't clear if this apparatus would also appear black in a color photograph. Center: you are standing with your hair pinned up wearing white undergarments. Behind you stands a man who is no doubt trying to close the hooks of your bra. One can only guess, for the picture has cut off both people at the chest, transforming them into two torsi. The man's tight-fitting shirt looks like a thin skin through which one can feel the warmth of his flesh. Bottom: you are seated in a wheelchair surrounded by two men and a woman. You are wearing a wool jacket and a long skirt, and a striped blanket lies on your lap. A scarf frames your pale face. Have you been frozen, or are you just frustrated?

Page twenty-one. Top: in your arms you are holding a bald baby doll with hollow eyes. Your throat is encircled by a piece of jewelry that reminds me of a collar for dogs. Have you ever been a dog? Center: you are standing beside a dark-haired woman and clinking glasses with her. Your makeup draws the outside corners of your eyes and lips slightly upward. Only at this point did I notice that to the right of each picture the title of the film was indicated. *Zig zig*: this still was from a film I'd never seen. I only knew that in this film you were called Marie. Bottom: you rest your cheek against the shoulder of a man wearing a dark sweater.

Page twenty-four. Top: two transparent water jugs, four glasses of white wine, two plates. You are sitting at a table with a young man whose face is repeated in a mirror. The man is holding a fork in his hand and is looking at you while you intertwine your fingers and lower your eyes. Center: you are standing out-of-doors with a man. In front of you, the shoulders of other people are visible. A strong wind is blowing from the front, shaping your hair into a mane. Bottom: with both hands you are holding a pistol in front of you. Your blouse clings to your skin. Behind you is a wall with cracks in it.

Between the pages of photographs there were other pages with a text in two voices. The voice printed in boldface said little, and almost always ended with a question mark, so this person must have been filled with despair during the conversation. The other voice never asked a question and spoke in larger blocks of text.

If only I had a dictionary! A few days later I saw a man in the city wearing a Russian shirt, a *rubashka*, offering yellowed books for sale. I stopped short, catching a glimpse of the Cyrillic characters on his table. Between Bakunin and Kropotkin lay a French-Russian dictionary. When I saw the price penciled inside its cover, no higher than the price of a crêpe, I couldn't help laughing in delight. The man looked at me angrily as though I'd insulted him.

My life and Marie's intersected only once a day. During the daytime I studied my textbook *Ecran* in the basement, which protected me from the sun's brutal spotlight. Marie slept until noon, got up silently and then went to buy us two crêpes, bananas, or Chinese food from a snack bar. In the late afternoon, I would make my way to one of the cinemas while Marie hurried off to work.

•

I looked up every single word in the dictionary as I read the dialogue in *Ecran*. So my progress was slow. The voice printed in boldface: "Ask—very—original—for—begin: how—are—you—begun—in—cinema? You—?—fifteen—years—, I—think." This annoyed me. I discovered that the bold voice often said "you" but spoke the word "I" only once in nine large pages, while the voice printed in large blocks of delicate script very often began a sentence with "I."

When I happened to walk past a stationer's and saw pens, envelopes, and glue in the window, I would imagine writing a letter to my parents. In the letter I would write that I was studying at a university in Paris and therefore couldn't come back home yet.

A long time had passed since I'd given Jörg my letter. Had he really sent it?

I lacked the opportunity, courage, and expertise to make serious inquiries as to how one went about getting admitted to the university. Instead of taking steps in this direction, I continued to stay curled up like a shrimp on a piece of cardboard in the basement, waiting for it to be late enough for me to go to the movies once more. Perhaps one could tell just by looking at me that I had thought too long and hard about becoming a student: One time I was given a student discount at the theater box office without even having asked for it.

Chapter Three

Tristana

The first time I saw the film *Tristana*, I exited the movie theater onto the dark sidewalk and saw a young, Vietnamese-looking woman about ten meters away. She was accompanied by a white-haired man, a Frenchman no doubt. I stepped to one side to keep the streetlight from illuminating my face, intending to wait there a moment until the two had passed. But the woman came right up to me and seized me by the elbow, talking like a sudden downpour. Caught off guard, I shook my head, trying to get away from her, or from her words. Her grip on my arm tightened; she kept trying to look into my eyes. Her mouth opened and closed like the mouth of a carp. Then her voice flooded into my ears—this was painful—and the meanings of the words stumbled behind, shamelessly taking hold of me. It was Ai Van, the woman with whom I'd shared the compartment on the night train to Paris. I wanted to explain why I hadn't gotten in touch with her, but she didn't let me speak. "So you're still in Paris! What splendid news! How have you been? Look how thin you've gotten." She took my hands, shaking them with each question. "Are you still just sightseeing? No, probably not. What have you been up to?" "I've been trying to find a way to study at the university, but it hasn't been working." "Where are you staying?" "With strangers." "Then you might as well come live with us. Perhaps we can find some way for you to receive a scholarship." Ai Van explained something in French to the white-haired man, who had been silent all this time. The man gave me a paternal nod. "Let me introduce you to my husband, this is Jean." Then she fell silent, obviously unable to remember my name. Maybe I'd never told it to her. Suddenly I felt uneasy about pronouncing my own name and gave a false one: "My name is Anh Nguyet."

Ai Van suggested I come with her at once and spend the night at their apartment. I found myself drawn into the melody of her speech, there was no chance for me to strike another note.

The room in which I spent this and many additional nights on a sofa was separated from the couple's bedroom by a thick, white wall. The wall was so white I couldn't fall asleep. I could hear every sound from the next room: pajamas rustling, smacking lips, soft plastic-slippered footsteps, masculine snoring. When I closed my eyes, I could hear the shadow-men from *Repulsion* gasping inside the wall.

Daylight arrived. A machine on the street was making a grinding sound. Something was scraping against hard material. Somewhere someone was opening a shop door with a metal grating. A car's engine started. A pigeon. Bottles clinking. Slippered footsteps in the hall. The shower. The coffee-maker. The clatter of silverware. A monotonous voice on the radio.

Ai Van and Jean did not exchange a single word during breakfast. I felt my neck tense up when Ai Van asked how my husband was. "I called him a while ago, and he told me he had a new girlfriend and there was no reason for me to go back." While I was uttering this lie, my eyes glazed over with tears. Ai Van heaved a sigh filled with pity. She pursed her lips in my direction and promised she would do something to help me. She wanted to arrange a fellowship for me to study at a language school as it was vital to learn the language regardless of what one intended to study.

I couldn't get Marie out of my mind. I asked Ai Van to write a letter in French. Ai Van immediately went to Jean's study to get a Mont Blanc fountain pen and stationery with a watermark in the shape of a swan. "Dear Marie, I am living with a countrywoman of mine who wants to help me find a language school. Thank you for everything you did for me. I will get in touch with you as soon as I have learned the language." This was the first and last written correspondence Marie received from me.

In truth, I didn't want to have breakfast with Ai Van and Jean. I would have much preferred to sit alone at the table later in the day and eat the hard brown tips of the croissants Ai Van always left behind on her plate, and drink tap water. Instead, Ai Van always woke me up and quickly set the table with three breakfast plates and three large coffee cups for *café au lait*. I felt ashamed that I was incapable of drinking coffee without putting in at least four cubes of sugar. I also felt guilty because Jean would stare off into space, embarrassed, whenever Ai Van told me a long story in Vietnamese. I didn't feel any need to converse with Ai Van over breakfast. My stomach could no longer endure the language whose meaning I understood. When I was silent and looked away, Ai Van would start chattering even more vivaciously. While she continued talking without pause she observed every movement of my fingers. When I put the croissant down on my plate she would immediately ask if it didn't taste good to me today. I would quickly respond, "Oh, it's very good," and go on eating. Whenever I picked up my coffee cup Ai Van would immediately say, "Careful, it's hot!" But when I stopped drinking and just listened to her for a while she would say, "Your coffee's getting cold."

Ai Van said she was a film student, but she was actually just trying to prepare for a film school's entrance exam despite the fact that she scarcely found time to study. Occasionally she would flip through a book with photographs of actors and actresses on its cover. Ai Van's fingers would lovingly stroke the faces depicted in the book, then she would continue flipping through the pages. Sometimes Jean would stand behind her and touch her hand. Ai Van would stretch her head back, her spine would arch, and her flaming tongue would tremble in the air like the tongue of a lizard attempting to intercept its prey mid-flight. Jean's tongue would dart out to play with hers. This game could continue for a long time while the forgotten pages of the books upon her desk slowly faded.

Jean was a lawyer. Sometimes he had to go to the office late in the evening or on weekends. Some days he could stay home. Whenever Jean left the house Ai Van would rise from her desk. The vacuum cleaner would be pressed into service, its droning buzz disturbing the quiet I needed to study. The vacuum ruthlessly sucked up every bit of knowledge that had accumulated on the desk along with the dust. Then Ai

Van would pluck the withered leaves from the flowers in the vase, hunt for missing socks, or scrub the dirty stovetop. Soon there was no longer anything that required her attention and she would return to her desk. As a housewife, however, she had invisible antennae like those of an insect that were constantly sensing new tasks in the air. For this reason she could not sit still for very long. Do we still have enough salt in the salt shaker? Ai Van retrieved a box of salt from the cupboard and filled the tiny container. The white powder whistled and glittered as time ran through her fingers.

Jean came home with a bouquet of roses. "Is it your birthday?" I asked Ai Van. "No, today is …" Then she whispered something in French and giggled, while her eyes sought Jean's approval. I saw age spots on the back of his hand. Instead of commenting, Jean stroked the back of his own head and let his nose stick out in the air a little. Somehow people who project happiness look a little like dogs.

Ai Van was proud of Jean. When he wasn't home, she sang his praises: a man like that, with broad shoulders, tall, well educated, who earned quite a bit of money. He was so terribly in love with her that he often couldn't concentrate on his work. At its worst he would simply cancel important appointments with his clients and come home early with his loins on fire. He said sweet things about her at every opportunity and never missed a chance to take her to a *fête* so that people could get a look at her. "A *fête*?" I asked, suddenly feeling agitated. "Isn't that what the Americans call a party, and doesn't the word 'party' mean the Communist Party as well?" I don't know what made me think of that. Ignoring my association, Ai Van blew her nose loudly and went on: "Today is the birthday of one of Jean's friends. Would you like to come along?" "I can't today. Today I've got to go to the movies," I said. "What a coincidence! You go to the movies every day." "But today it's especially important."

I missed the smell of Marie's perfume, her perfume that used to pierce my nostrils like a toxin. I missed the delicate airborne particles of dust that used to appear in the shaft of morning light slanting down into the basement. I couldn't talk about these things with Ai Van.

Ai Van kneaded her own flesh into the shape of a woman she could present in public. She coordinated her hairstyle with her shoes, her smile with her lipstick, her fingers with her handbag. She glanced about almost coquettishly, yet no one would despise her, let alone laugh at her, for there was nothing ridiculous about her at all. If I were to stand before your poster at the cinema and start a conversation with your picture, people would laugh at me even though nothing was ridiculous about my actions. People would either laugh or walk past me in silence as if I weren't there. If I were to say at a party that the silver screen was the bed-sheet upon which I did all my living and sleeping, no one would want to talk to me anymore. I had never been to a party. Ai Van explained to me that a party was a place where you could show off your lover or husband and tell stories about your vacation. "So you really don't want to come?" Ai Van was using a silver shoehorn to insert her feet into particularly tall high-heeled shoes. "No, I really do have to go to the movies today." Jean was already standing outside the apartment door, groaning with impatience.

I was in bed already when Ai Van and Jean returned from the birthday party. At first I heard footsteps on the stairs, then the door opened, a whispering crept into the apartment, followed by irregular steps in the hall. The water faucet turned on. The rustle of fabric. Steel springs creaking in the mattress. And breathing, breathing, breathing.

In the early morning hours Jean appeared to resist pro-tracted physical contact with Ai Van. He would hold her face between his hands and kiss her carefully and conserva-tively upon the lips while she attempted to press her entire body against his. "I always need skin contact. The only people who can understand this are ones who grew up in a tropical climate like we did." Ai Van expected me to agree with her, but I couldn't identify with this tropical skin lust. "Wouldn't you say the climate I grew up in was more Communist than tropical?" "No, you are a tropical human being, just like me. Jean is completely different, because the air in Paris stays cool and dry for months at a time." "But in the summer it's hot here, too." "Summer doesn't count. It's winter that makes people who they are."

Jean was a lawyer, but he wasn't always able to use law to help people. One day Ai Van asked him to help a relative of hers who lived in Marseille. He had loaned money to a native Frenchman that had never been repaid. I met this relative one day when he visited us in Jean's absence. He was an angular man with a hoarse voice. When he sat down on the sofa, I noticed that his right leg didn't bend. He responded to my look of surprise with a disarming smile and rolled up his trousers to show me his prosthetic leg. A cousin of mine had been given a similar leg after he'd lost his old one to a landmine.

Ai Van's question for Jean was lengthy. I certainly would not have understood it had she not translated it for me. Jean's answer was monosyllabic: "Non." I was happy because for the first time I completely understood what he said. Ai Van's face turned stony. After a while she tried to appeal to his reason and at the same time repair his heart; he, meanwhile, withdrew behind the curtains of his face. Later Ai Van translated Jean's justification for his refusal: It was problematic when the client was in precarious financial circumstances.

Jean could not work for free as it was forbidden. And if the client happened to be lacking a legal residence permit, Jean could be charged with supporting an illegal entity. Ai Van couldn't believe that her husband, who never hesitated to buy her dresses and earrings, would deny such an urgent request. "Illegal, you say? He isn't an illegal person, he's my relative!" Jean added sympathetically that even if he were to take the case, the man might be arrested instead of getting his money back. It wasn't possible to call attention to one's rights without displaying one's dirty laundry as well. A lawyer had no power to bend the law.

Ai Van went back to bed after Jean left for work. I went to the movies so as not to have to remain alone with her in a single room. In the snack shop attached to the cinema I studied the flyers and programs that were scattered around, looking for a film in which you appear.

"Tristana": The color of this name is brown. The drone of church bells drags each letter of this name down with it. On the screen, the air takes on the hue of autumn leaves. Even your hair is brunette this time. Human beings live through four seasons, like trees. Our hair changes color like leaves.

You've had your hair woven into two braids. The way you look reminds me of a girl in a Communist youth organization or, better yet, in an old French children's book. Your name is Tristana. You use your fingers and lips to speak with a boy who is deaf and dumb. You will be able to speak with me as well.

A paternal figure, Don Lope, pulls the girl Tristana to him and presses his rotting lips against hers. The girl laughs like a broken windup doll. I too used to laugh like this when I felt ill at ease. Don Lope's face still wears its serious/sexual expression; he is refusing to loosen the reins. My grandfather used to say that even an eighty-year-old man can still learn things from an eighty-one-year-old, as human beings grow wiser with each year.

It was particularly late when I returned from the movies that night. Standing in the kitchen, Ai Van told me that Jean still wasn't back yet. He'd come home earlier, but the argument had flared up again. Ai Van had jabbed him with her elbow as he tried to bite off her earlobe. He'd fallen awkwardly backwards, striking his head against the edge of the sideboard. "Murderers, every one of you! The war went on too long, it's driven all of you mad!" he shrieked in a magpie voice. Without thinking, Ai Van reached for a jar of jam and hurled it at his mouth. She wanted to run out of the apartment, but Jean was faster.

Jean and Ai Van drank their coffee without a word. In the milk foam I could see my desire to leave them. I remembered the warmth of the paper cups Marie had brought back to the basement room with her. To Marie I was perhaps nothing more than a little blister on her skin that didn't hurt much but didn't mean anything either. I had to earn some income of my own before I returned to her. I was surely not a burden to Ai Van. On the contrary. She needed me to establish a united female front against Jean. She enjoyed looking after me. Every day, like the mother of a thirteen-year-old girl, she would ask: "Where are you going?" "To the movies." "Again? Are you going by yourself?" "Of course. I don't know anyone. I don't speak French." "Why do you go to the movies if you don't speak French?" I didn't reveal to her that Tristana had her own language of signs and therefore was able to communicate without the use of her tongue.

I saw the film for a second time. As a child I would read a book so often that the pages flew out of it. Why shouldn't I keep watching a movie until the screen was in tatters? I felt guilty seeing a film for the second time. Ai Van always looked perfectly content when she opened her wallet to give me pocket money, but I felt as if I were betraying her.

Tristana makes the acquaintance of a painter. And right away the bell that swings in the tower of the church is transformed into the head of Don Lope. Who chopped his head off and hung it there? Perhaps a girl who is shy can become an insolent murderer in her dreams. Would the judge then refer to the case of *Repulsion* and say that the murderer might repeat her crime? In reality, *Tristana* is not condemned to death. She doesn't even get arrested, for old Don Lope is still alive. He is immortal, as is often the case with actors. He stares into a mirror, carefully grooming his beard. Dry bits of food and saliva cling to the hairs—his beard is the second-rate pubic hair of men. Along with his accessories, including his beard, cigars, and hat, he goes into a bar filled with exclusively male amusement-seekers. The men wear black top hats and spit out jokes from the pudendal crevices hidden in their beards. Sometimes they burst into communal laughter, but even then their eyes remain cold and malicious.

A dog is standing on a street corner that is strangely cut off from the city. The city's inhabitants are uneasy because they are unable to pinpoint the location of the dog. The dog is mad and enraged; it is lonesome and delicately boned.

One of Tristana's legs is amputated. The leg that has been cut off turns into a wooden leg that lies on the narrow bed as if it were just tossed there. Tristana has assumed a facial expression reminiscent of a piece of furniture carved of ebony. Perhaps we all are on our way to becoming pieces of furniture in order to make everything more tolerable. Then we are locked in an interior containing a camera. Only the rabid dog is free, for no one knows where it is. Perhaps the dog was spliced into this film by accident.

Rather than knocking on the door, the deaf-and-dumb boy throws a rock at the second floor window behind which Tristana is undressing. The window opens like an altar, and Tristana displays herself in a morning coat. Beneath the coat she is naked. The boy moves his hands as if he were taking off a morning coat. Tristana copies his gesture. The boy steps back, trembling, his eyes wide open, he steps backward into the bushes as if someone were rewinding the film.

Jean's eyes lingered on the autumn leaves outside the kitchen window while his lips still searched for a good spot on his coffee cup. Ai Van cried out: "Watch out! You're spilling!" Jean gave a start, and a brown drop fell on his white shirt. The spot enlarged like the pupils of a cat that has stepped into a dark room. "It's going into the washing machine anyhow," Jean remarked, annoyed, and left the table. I, too, got up and quickly left the room. "Where are you going?" Ai Van employed this question to detain me. "To the movies." "At this hour?" "To the ten o'clock matinee. They start showing movies at nine," I responded hastily, retracing my steps and sitting back down beside her. Before she could start in on her litany of complaints about Jean, I asked if he already had a beard when he was young. Ai Van smiled ironically. "When Jean was young, I wasn't even born yet." "But it is surely advantageous when a man has reached the age of maturity." Ai Van drew her eyebrows together. Behind her I saw the second hand of the wall clock stumbling forward. "You have the wrong idea about older men. There are some that have remained capable of reproduction. Sometimes they are even stiffer than the younger ones." "I meant that they are emotionally mature." "Jean is still a child. If we had a real child, maybe things would be different. Jean hates children. He can't even enjoy eating at a restaurant if there's a family with a child at the next table." The conversation was developing in an unexpected direction, and my head began to fill with Tristana's sand-colored world. "I've had some of Jean's sperm frozen. When he is dead, I'm going to have it defrosted and inserted in my uterus." "But then the child would be fatherless from the very beginning." "Oh, nowadays it's normal for children not to have a father. Jean will make his contribution as a father in the form of an inheritance. I don't want to burden him with children. As long as he's alive, let him enjoy life."

"You've spilled again," Ai Van exclaimed. Jean tore the shirt from his body, displaying the chest hair sticking out from the semicircular neckline of his undershirt. Then he took off his trousers as well. I fled from the sight of his hairy legs. Ai Van blanched, and Jean closed the door of his study behind him so quietly it was almost eerie.

Ai Van made us green tea and began to tell me about her father. He, too, had studied law, but since he didn't think he would be able to have any sort of career in Vietnam, he resolved in 1975 to leave the country. I felt the anger of former times awaken within me and said: "If all the intelligent people had left the country, there would have been no one left to improve it. There would never have been any Doimoi politics, no reforms." Ai Van responded, her voice filled with venom: "And why did you leave the country? If you really loved your country so much, you never would have left."

There was a scene in the film *Tristana* where the workers threw stones at men wearing uniforms and then ran away. I didn't know the time period or the city in which the story was set, but apparently class struggle existed there as well. The lens of the camera was on the side of the poor. Isn't this why Don Lope was always shown in such an unattractive light while the deaf-mute and the impecunious painter appeared so simpatico? What would things have looked like if the camera lens had chosen to show the world the other way around? And what if I could see the same way without the help of the camera? But that would be impossible— without the camera's lens I would never have the chance to see these people.

Tristana was one of the paupers, and unfortunately this character was being played by you, making Tristana so beautiful that the rich man would never leave her in peace.

Tristana flees from her marriage on two legs and comes back on one. Then she continues her life with the rich Don Lope. One evening while a snowstorm is acting crazy, Don

Lope has a heart attack. Is it itself a form of class struggle when Tristana opens the bedroom window instead of calling the doctor, so that the sick old man freezes to death?

"What movie did you see?" Ai Van asked. I hesitated with my response. "You're hiding something from me. Do you sometimes watch indecent films?" If I hadn't paid the admission with Ai Van's money, I wouldn't have felt obligated to tell her about the movies. "Luis Buñuel," I answered quickly so as not to reveal your name. Ai Van knew of this director and told me about another film of his with the title *Terre sans pain* that she had recently seen with Jean. "Jean was horrified that poverty was being depicted so blatantly. It was a documentary, set in a village in Spain in the 1930s. The people were just lying about as if paralyzed, and yet only their poverty was to blame, nothing else. The end of the film was propagandistic, the messages were even spelled out in letters, not just shown in pictures: 'Comrade, rise to your feet for the Revolution' or something of the sort. Jean was shocked. I already knew more or less what poverty looked like."

One week later, Ai Van and Jean began to eat croissants with jam. At night I sometimes heard a series of vigorous noises emanating from their bedroom. Not every night, not even every fourth night, but precisely every third. Apparently everyday life had been restored. The stuffed rabbit in my room looked browner and more naked than ever. Its nose, made of a soft synthetic material, was gradually decomposing.

Ai Van failed to keep her promise to find a way for me to study. Perhaps she needed to have me at home, in case she ever had to battle Jean again. Jean was friendly toward me. At least I never had the sense I was disturbing him. I was a few years younger than Ai Van, he said to me, and he was much older than she was. He wanted me to think of him as a father, Ai Van translated for me with a superior smile in her eyes.

"Do you think there's still a chance for me to enroll in a language school?" "As far as I'm concerned, you can do so right away. But are you sure it's the right thing for you?" In Ai Van's eyes, I was a girl with holes in my mouth. To protect oneself from cavities was easy enough, but these holes in my organ of speech were incurable. "You aren't a natural at speaking; I think it would be better for you to learn some sort of handicraft that requires a great deal of patience. Patience you have." "I like to talk." "Your lips are a good shape for sucking, not speaking." "That's not true. I learned Russian." "That's not a real language." "Why not?" "It's incomprehensible." "I'll leave this apartment next week if you don't bring me some information about language schools." "Blackmail? Well, all right. I'll see what I can do."

I was under the impression that a language school would solve every one of my problems in a single blow. The simple sentence: "I am studying in Paris" would wipe from my body all suspicion of being a prostitute, an illegal alien, a thief, imposter, or fraud. Studying in Paris was most certainly a refined occupation. Even Ho Chi Minh spent six years studying here. In Moscow, on the other hand, he studied only one year. My uncle told me that once to tease me. Now I was grateful to him for this information.

Chapter Four

The Hunger

Jean was drinking tomato juice. Ai Van went into the bathroom and didn't return right away. "This tastes good," I think Jean said, and I found myself fascinated by the pale, dry skin on the back of his hand that, because of the particular way the light was striking it, appeared almost transparent. My fingers flew over the absent wife's teacup to stroke the old skin, then gave it a firm pinch. Jean shouted and grabbed my fingers, pulling them to his mouth, and bit down. I screamed. "What's going on?" Ai

Van jumped out of the bathroom; I hid my throbbing hand behind my back, got up, and peered at my right eye in the mirror as if looking for an insect.

A year had passed without my ever having spent time alone with Jean. Perhaps Ai Van made a point of never leaving us alone. I, too, avoided being alone with him whenever possible. When I was home, Ai Van stayed home as well. When Ai Van left the house, I made sure I went out as well, usually to the movies, since I didn't know where else to go. In the movie theaters there were sometimes men who spoke to me. I would say a word that didn't exist in any language and walk away. This one word was meant to signify: "I am unable to speak." It was a noun in the singular signifying "speechless subject"; or else it was a verb that could be used only in the first person singular and meant the opposite of "to speak."

Sometimes I would flip through the dictionary Ai Van had given me to translate more of the text from *Ecran*. The dialogue piece was an interview with you. The letters crept off the paper and were being taken over by your voice. But every time Ai Van came into my room, the words quickly retreated into the dictionary's shell, making me feel abandoned.

"I want to work in a factory." "In a factory? Can't you think of a better job?" "What would be a better job?" "Why don't you want to work in a café, for example." "It's dishonorable to work as a waitress, a waitress is obliged to serve customers." "What's wrong with that?" "It's the same as the nobility and colonial masters who had servants at home to serve them meals. And it's completely ridiculous when customers pay some piddling tip just so they can play the role of this extinct ruling class." "But there's only self-service in cheap fast-food restaurants and the student cafeteria." "Expensive restaurants should use self-service too, then people will start to understand." "If there were no more waitresses, a lot of people would lose their jobs." "There are many other meaningful forms of work. They simply aren't being offered as jobs." "You are still completely obsessed with these strange ideas. Didn't you see how the Berlin Wall fell? That was over a year ago now." "How could I have seen that? I wasn't in Berlin." "I mean on television, of course." "I don't watch television. Television programs have nothing to do with my life." "You don't have a life. You go to the movies, and besides that you don't do anything at all." "That's why I want to work in a factory." "It's so difficult for people without an education to find work. And you lack not only an education but the ability to speak the language. Perhaps it really would be better for you to do factory work. But I don't know anyone who works in a factory. What about housecleaning?" "That would be great, too."

I'd heard that some of the greatest celebrities cleaned other people's homes and offices for work when they were young. When you clean, you see what people consume and throw away. This gives you a good grasp of the national economy. A woman should always begin her career as a housecleaner. I couldn't remember if these words of wisdom came from Confucius, Ho Chi Minh, or someone else. I found them quite plausible. "What I'd really like to do would be to clean houses for movie stars." "That's nonsense. A person who wants to work must begin by setting aside his own wishes and going wherever he is sent."

Jean didn't seem to approve of my plan. He spent half an hour arguing glumly with Ai Van. Later she told me Jean was worried. He was afraid that if I got a job, someone might find out I was living here illegally. Then Jean and Ai Van could be held responsible for having harbored a visaless creature for over a year. "Does this mean I won't be able to work or even show my face for the rest of my life?" Ai Van's nostrils expanded as she smiled in embarrassment. "Jean thinks we should stage an accident that would solve everything. A car runs you over and damages your memory. You can speak Vietnamese, but you no longer recall anything from your past. Then they'll send you home, and none of us will be held responsible."

There was a job for me. Ai Van whispered these words quietly into my ear although Jean wasn't even home. A private clinic was looking for someone. I was to go there three times a week; the salary would be satisfactory even though the work was quite easy. I found this offer far preferable to throwing myself in front of a car and feigning amnesia.

It was a Monday. The clinic was situated on the outskirts of town. Beneath a gray sky, I walked at a rapid pace between immense concrete warehouses. Large trucks passed, no drivers visible in their elevated front seats. Except for me, the sidewalk was completely empty. Only once did I cross paths with another persona—a tall slender African.

As instructed, I rang the bell by the door that displayed the three letters "C.S.L." A young woman in a white lab coat welcomed me, led me to one of the back rooms, and introduced me to Dr. Lee. This Chinese doctor was from Hanoi and had spent time in Bangkok as well. Dr. Lee had never been to China, but hoped to go some day to collect snake skins. She moved to Paris ten years ago. At first she occupied herself with plastic surgery for the victims of accidents and wars, and became particularly well-known for her skill at concealing facial scars. Then she began to take on additional assignments in general plastic surgery, as well as collecting medicinal herbs and developing products to repel mosquitoes and cockroaches. She was also developing a line of cosmetics and diet pills. My task was to allow her to use my skin for experiments.

Dr. Lee marked off the area to be tested with lipstick on the soft, sensitive skin of my inside left arm. Then she rubbed three different salves on my skin.

When I returned to the clinic two days later, one area

of my skin was red. Dr. Lee studied this area with her magnifying glass, scraped off a bit of skin and examined it under her microscope. Then she asked me if I'd ever given blood. "Of course. Why do you ask?" She extracted a thick cylinder of blood from me and smeared a salve where the needle had entered. This wound became infected two days later.

The clinic employed several women whom I only ever saw from behind. On my third visit, I was paid for the first time. I was told to eat a lot of spinach and inner organs before I returned the following week.

With the cash in my pocket I went to the movies. For the first time, I paid for my ticket with my own money.

During fifteen minutes spent in a hospital waiting room, the skin can lose its color and acquire countless tiny folds. Beneath the eyes, little pockets of flesh collect; the lips grow dry and the hair falls out. These things might happen during a short wait. The sort of perfectly ordinary short wait I experienced constantly: waiting for the light to turn green, for the next métro to arrive, for my turn in line at the movie theater. I waited for things hundreds of times every single day, though only for very short periods of time. Even during these infinitesimal spans of time, the body can be transformed, slip through a hole in time, and re-emerge a century later. My blood supply would run out eventually, just as every movie has to end. Even eating the undercooked flesh of animals, drinking tomato juice, eating bright red borscht, and biting into pomegranates cannot prevent the blood from growing thinner and thinner.

In this film your name is Miriam. Miriam is a vampire. Your partner, a vampire in baroque makeup who flutters his thick eyelashes like a rock star, suddenly ages while waiting in a hospital. Miriam places his coffin on a stage where no more rock concerts will take place. Other coffins are already onstage.

After her partner's death, Miriam gazes deep into the eyes of a young woman in a white lab coat. The woman is surprised by this vampire gaze, for usually she only looks at the skulls of monkeys on a screen. She seems to be a biologist.

Miriam offers the biologist a glass of red wine. They clink glasses and drink with trembling fingers. The young woman splashes wine on her blouse and takes it off. First her bosom is bared, then her hips and legs. Standing confidently in front of naked science is Miriam, the champion of the blood-sucker clan. She removes her black undergarments as well. The two female bodies lie down together on the bed, four hands stroking, pressing, rubbing, two mouths open, searching, sucking, and the air is silken. While I, the movie-goer, dream transfixed, and the biologist falls asleep as if freshly in love, Miriam kisses science on her weak spot. Blood is sucked, a mark remains behind, and a new vampire is born.

Ai Van warned me not to tell Jean about my new job yet. He would definitely be opposed. The man who had given us the information about the job was the same man from Marseille with the prosthetic leg. For this reason Ai Van and I discussed the job only in Jean's absence. "How are things at the clinic?" "They told me I should eat a lot of inner organs and spinach," I reported hesitantly, for Ai Van hated to take other's requests into account concerning food. There were always arguments when Jean made comments about the food, such as "It's a bit too salty" or "Are there only vegetables in this soup?" Up till now I had always eaten everything Ai Van cooked for us without remark. "Inner organs and spinach? They don't know what they're talking about. They probably want you to produce blood more quickly. For that one should drink turtle blood. Snake blood would work well too. Both are difficult to find here. If you're lucky, you can get snakes and turtles at a specialty shop for book binders, but not a grocer's." "Isn't there any substitute?" "Well, maybe *foie gras* would be good for you." "What's that?" "You really don't know? How long have you been living here?" "Do you think I'm going to have to keep giving blood?" "I don't know." "Have you gone through the same thing?" "No, of course not." "What will happen to me if I keep losing blood?" "New blood is constantly produced." "But my blood, the blood that was inside me, is no longer there." "It's better to rid yourself of old blood. Otherwise you'll age more quickly."

That evening Ai Van made us coalfish with potatoes and cabbage. As Jean ate in silence, I discovered a minute trace of lipstick on his white collar.

It is time to suck out the blood of the victim—the man Miriam has seduced at a disco and brought home with her. His jeans don't fit so well. He has a crumpled grin, and his head is filled with one thought: perhaps this incredibly beautiful woman will allow me ..., I might ..., maybe I'll ..., and perhaps these fleshy curves ..., and so on. He is embraced, pressed against the wall, and emptied out. A scream that comes too late, a rescue that never comes. He is consumed and tossed to one side—a snack for Miriam.

The biologist is not a snack; she is the partner Miriam has chosen. Miriam lovingly sucks her blood to make her one of them. After the ritual she will cease her scientific explorations of nature and will be a vampire. Will she have trouble adjusting to this change of profession?

Even at an early age, as a young woman named Carol working at a beauty salon, you were beginning to practice for your future profession. Carol cleans the fingernails of an elegant lady. A close-up showing the pale surface of this lady's skin reveals thin body hair and droplets of sweat. Carol is distracted by thoughts of the shadow man from the night before. The nail scissors slip from her hand into the deadly dream, into the woman's flesh. The jaws of the screaming woman with their formidable teeth fill the screen, viscous blood flows out, shiny and black.

At night I would sneak out of the house to return to the movie theater. I was like a boat adrift, and the gleaming marquees were lighthouses. Most of the passersby looked as if they'd just left a restaurant. I had never once eaten in a restaurant in this city. Nor did I pay the slightest attention to the menus posted outside the restaurants, for I knew I would never find your name there.

In Vietnam, vampires appeared only metaphorically. Interest rates, for example, were seen as vampires, since they sucked the blood of the people and grew fatter and fatter. Entrepreneurs and drug dealers were described as vampires as well. In Paris, on the other hand, that is, in the movie theater, real vampires could be found. They were not metaphorical. I no longer had any objection to becoming a vampire—being completely emptied out, belonging, sharing blood in order to survive, surviving in togetherness. With Miriam. Life as a vampire might even be preferable to my current one. I wanted to become a vampire. When I'd had enough prey, I would immediately extract blood from my arm with a thick syringe and fill Miriam's wineglass. Actually both the syringe and the wineglass were superfluous. Miriam would drink directly from my neck—a pleasure for me.

Miriam plays the role of a bourgeois lady living in an elegantly furnished apartment who gives children music lessons. She doesn't really need to earn any money as the form of nourishment she requires cannot be bought with money. The cost is not money, but rather blood and flesh. Miriam, however, cannot afford to become conspicuous. A person who does not work immediately stands out. Perhaps there are many who work only for this reason. When I started work at the clinic, I began to walk right in the middle of the sidewalk. I no longer hung my head, my hands stopped looking for an invisible railing in the air. I no longer had cause to feel guilty. I was working, I was a worker, I was no longer nobody.

The enviable woman whom Miriam has selected cannot grasp how fortunate she is. Perhaps the sciences have no vocabulary for describing the happiness one feels as a vampire. She is confused; she wanders about with a distraught expression and disheveled hair, arrives panting in front of a telephone, attempts to dial a number, sweating profusely, apparently trying to salvage something. Is she crazed because she's drunk the blood of her own husband? What a shame he's dead, but his death isn't her fault—it's just the vampire lifestyle. When people eat chicken fricassee, the chicken is also dead. She must be afraid of something else. In her previous life she conducted experiments on monkeys to study abnormal phenomena in nature. Now she herself has become a phenomenon that is not rationally comprehensible. If a biologist were to wake up one morning as a laboratory rat, she would immediately commit suicide. I would go on living as a rat until a human killed me.

Every vampire wears a necklace that is really a knife. You have to use this knife to cut open the neck of your victim and siphon off the blood to drink. The teeth of modern-day vampires are not sharp enough to pierce the skin. Miriam wears such a knife, and the biologist does as well. She stabs the knife into her own neck. She screams, bleeds to death, and dies. What are you doing?! Why are you doing this?! Miriam collapses in tears. There is no return.

She no longer exists. But what "she" is it that has vanished? There is still the face of the biologist who no longer works in her laboratory but instead gives children music lessons. Has Miriam put on the body of the dead researcher like a stage costume? Or is it in fact Miriam who has died? The two women have become one.

Chapter Five

Indochine

A melody ripples across the screen, muddy water fills my field of vision. Ships with dragon wings are being navigated and rowed by Vietnamese-looking men and women. A few seconds later your name appears in pink letters. As always, this is the breathtaking climax of the film. Before the title is revealed and the story begins, your name must emerge from beneath the sea. Without this name there would be no actress, and without her there would be no Eliane Devries, who is supposed to have lived in Indochina, and without Eliane there would be no story to tell. The only Indochina I've ever seen was on the screen in Paris.

The narrating voice belonged to you. I didn't understand what was being said, but I recognized your voice. And because I didn't understand, the voice floated on its own, self-confident, elastic, rising and falling. I heard breathing, friction, sighs, sometimes even ardor becoming sound. This was the first time you spoke in a film before showing yourself. Your voice rising from the water, the sails, the wind, the rubber trees.

Someone is already dead before the story begins. Your voice speaks of this deceased person. Eliane stands before an altar in a mourning dress, a black veil hangs over her face. Beside her stands a little girl who has not yet reached a third of her full height. The girl takes Eliane's hand without looking up, as if it is her self-evident right to do so. The girl's face expresses dignity, though her skin probably still bears the creases left behind by her diapers.

Eliane and the girl cannot be blood relatives. The girl bears a strong resemblance to someone. I can hardly believe my eyes, but the girl resembles me as I appear in a specific childhood photograph. I suspect the girl's parents are dead and Eliane has adopted her. The clothes and the atmosphere of the ceremony reveal the high social standing of the departed.

It was highly unlikely that my parents died after my departure, but when Ai Van asked me why I never wrote to them, I quickly replied that they were dead. The next day I realized that a death can never be taken back again, not even a fictional one.

Is the tango a contract between a man and a woman? Between a man whose warm muscles are palpable through the thin cloth of his trousers and a woman who allows herself to be twirled like a white silk glove? Is the tango a pantomime between a woman with provocative glances and a man whose thin lips never show the slightest hint of a smile?

Eliane and the Vietnamese girl, who is now approximately seventeen years old, dance the tango together in their living room. The sweetly undulating melody binds them together like lovers. With the movements of their chins, they challenge one another to a duel. When you dance the tango, you are not allowed to laugh, but these two laugh every time they stumble or fall on the sofa. Missteps are fun. This ballroom dance is taking place without a ballroom, for they are dancing all alone in their own living room. Thus everything is allowed. Another misstep. Who kicked whom? Eliane is the first to tumble to the sofa and is speechless for two seconds. Has Camille tossed her over her shoulder like a judo expert? Is this a martial art? Suddenly both of them collapse in communal laughter until they're out of breath.

The whip stops swinging. Eliane stands with the whip in her hand, and at her feet kneels an old plantation worker. He is wearing a tattered shirt and gazes up at Eliane with red eyes in which a sort of gratitude is trembling. Eliane speaks to him affectionately. The workers are her children—they must be loved, shielded, punished, and fed. The rubber trees behind her are like the columns of an invisible palace.

Eliane is eating mango with a spoon. She puts every other spoonful in the mouth of her adopted daughter, as if she were still a baby. One spoonful of mango for her own mouth, one for the mouth of Camille. Eating mango makes the body green inside. Eliane wants Camille to become just as green as she is. The curve of the spoon resembles a mother's breast, the roundness of buttocks or belly, but the spoon is cold. Camille's face would look distorted if mirrored in the spoon. Her face is no longer a child's face, nor does it bear any similarity to the face of Eliane.

I would like to eat a mango again. It's been five years since I've had one. Give me a bit of mango, too! Now! Me! Me!

Me! My language becomes childish when I speak to you. The words ramble around discretely, without a goal, my voice rises into the heights like a twittering bird, and suddenly I see you standing before me. Your eyelashes slant toward me in pity, your lips faintly follow mine when I speak, as if you were repeating my words. Truthfully, you are dubbing my story as you place one piece of mango after the other on my tongue. The juicy fruit fills the hollow of my mouth, and now I speak only French without understanding what I am saying.

You are wearing a modern dress that resembles a traditional Vietnamese *áo dài*. The straight lines of the narrow dress camouflage your shapely, feminine contours, giving you a figure like bamboo. Even your hair, which usually dances curly and golden in the air, has now been woven into an elegant nest. This is your way of adapting to the Southeast Asian landscape.

A boy and an old man, both wearing brown, tattered clothes, stand on a ramshackle sailboat. Apparently, they are being interrogated for something they've done. The Frenchmen in white uniforms refuse to accept their words, set fire to the sailboat, and push it away from the hull of their own boat. The two remain standing on the burning boat, making no attempt to defend themselves. The boat becomes smaller and smaller, or the landscape on the screen becomes larger and larger. Soon the only thing visible is a tiny flame flickering in the night sky.

"What movie did you see yesterday?" "I've forgotten already. It wasn't so interesting." "Not so interesting? But you go to the movies every day." "To pass the time." "But you have a job. Surely it must be exciting to work in that mysterious clinic." "Sometimes I feel dizzy. I'm short on blood." "You'll manage. You should try to earn as much as possible now that you are making good money. Soon you'll have enough saved to be able to go home." I tried to conceal my horror. For a long time, returning home had been my only wish. Now it felt like a trap.

Hats make the man. The natives are wearing cone-shaped straw hats, while the Frenchmen wear military caps or top hats. The hats of the French women are elegant: a different butterfly flutters on the top of each. When you change your hat, you change your identity. Jean-Baptiste takes off his navy hat and at once stops sacrificing himself for his fatherland. His soft hair clings to his damp forehead; his eyes have a wild, vulnerable gleam. What remains of his former pride now only fills him with rage. He is being hunted and pursued as a traitor. Once he was the little finger of his fatherland, entrusted with the task of saving the sinking colonial ship of Indochina. Now he is merely a chunk of enamored penis, that is, an individual. Again and again his skin gets wet: with rain, sweat or blood, tears, river water, amniotic fluid.

Jean-Baptiste never smiles, he never blushes or winks. He is a green papaya—he speaks passionately, furiously, nakedly to Eliane, while she looks off to one side coldly. One day he gets a nosebleed and falls to the ground. When Eliane bends over him to wipe his nose, he tries to pull her torso down to kiss her. But he's rejected. You are now Eliane, not Carol, not Tristana. As Miriam from the clan of the vampires, you might have drunk the blood of Jean-Baptiste. As Eliane you will inherit your father's plantation and raise an adopted daughter. You are a new woman whose acquaintance I must make.

On another day, Jean-Baptiste enters Eliane's house without knocking. He silently walks up to her and tries to capture her lips with his own. Or he dashes out of a casino, leaps into the car in which Eliane is seated, climbs on top of her and gropes her thighs. The Indian chauffeur gets out of the car, opens his big umbrella, and waits in the rain until the two finish wrestling.

At dawn the workers are striding between the trees. Tiny lamps are affixed to their foreheads; and in their hands they hold knives. At first glance, this march looks like an uprising; in truth these men are on their way to work. They will use their knives to cut into the skin of the rubber trees to collect the milky blood of the trees in containers. Nonetheless, the colonial regime will soon collapse.

Studying revolutions at school, I sometimes felt pity for the countries that had accidentally developed capitalist governments, forcing the people to play an unsavory role in history. Capitalism can sustain itself only by exploiting other countries, my teacher said. And so the first countries to develop capitalism were compelled to first exploit us and then feel ashamed, while we were always able to hold our heads up as Heroes of World History. If new wars were not always being waged, I wouldn't be demanding apologies from the miscreants of bygone eras. Inevitably, new situations constantly arise, each more secret and cruel than the last. As you play a role in a movie, I, too, play a role in History. Sometimes I wonder who's directing my film.

I used to have conversations with my girlfriends about how we should behave so as to be revolutionary. My mother, on the other hand, was not at all interested in revolutions; what interested her was the theater, romantic novels, and the love affairs of her neighbors and acquaintances. When, for example, we heard that a married woman had run off with her lover, my mother would remark with a sigh: "It was Buddha's will." I would contradict her: "Why should we do what Buddha wants? He may be Indian or Nepalese, but he certainly is not in charge of our nation!"

•

Yoko Tawada

Since Ai Van asked me several times over breakfast which film I had just seen, I finally revealed the title *Indochine*. The word sounded like a botched tofu dish. The movie was about neither India nor China—it was about us. How could they have come up with such a name?

Ai Van told me she'd just read something about this movie in a film magazine. Wanting to avoid telling her about the heroine's beauty, I gave a brief, objective summary of the film, adding that it offered a suitably critical look at the late-stage colonial period that paved the way for revolution. Ai Van's response was irritation. "It's easy to criticize colonialism. Freedom and independence, however, are French products, like *foie gras*." Jean, who usually kept out of our conversations, asked Ai Van what was going on. Ai Van translated what we'd said. Jean gave a bitter smile. "Vietnam was quick to go up in Communist flames. If France had behaved in a gentler, more adult way, perhaps the idea of independence wouldn't have fused with that of Communism. And then the Americans would have stayed away, there wouldn't have been any war, and Vietnam today would be at least as wealthy and peaceful as Thailand." When Ai Van translated this for me, the blood shot into my temples. "What nonsense! That is completely wrong! The flames shot out of the boat that the boy and the old man stood on! And who set the boat on fire? Not the Communists!" Jean seemed taken aback by my vehemence.

"What boat are you talking about?" "The boat in the movie." "Oh, I see. I haven't seen that film yet. But the French administration in Indochina was never as destructive as the Japanese one that preceded it. Besides, we later opposed the Vietnam War. It really might have been possible for Vietnam to develop into an industrial nation in cooperation with us, without Communism or the war. What a shame that things turned out so differently." I said: "Jean, don't you know that Ho Chi Minh always named independence and freedom in this order and never the other way around?" Ai Van laughed dryly instead of translating and asked, "Are you still in love with him?" Jean immediately wanted to know what I had said. Ai Van translated. He replied: "Independence is an abstraction. The main thing is to escape being murdered and become as rich as possible."

Enraged, I left the house. The street wasn't telling me which way to go. All I could think of was the word *cinéma*—the meeting place of "China" and "Ma." The entrance of the movie theater welcomed me like the arms of a "Ma." She never thrust me away, not even today, though I'd seen the same film three times already.

The red velvet cloth is removed, revealing a gramophone. The invited guests applaud, delighted. Even Eliane's face is beaming with joy. She asks Camille to dance the tango with her. Camille shakes her head no, but Eliane will not be deprived of this pleasure. Eliane gets up, takes off her jacket, and removes the silk shawl from Camille's shoulders. They dance, neck and arms bare, the two of them as one. Even their glances and gestures, admittedly reminiscent of a duel, are nonetheless signs of their inseparableness. The eyes of the guests are transfixed by the sight of the dancing couple. The Indian chauffeur is proud of his mistress and her daughter. A housemaid, too, is gazing at them with dreamy eyes, but she is soon shooed back to her task of fanning the gramophone, which otherwise might melt in the tropical heat.

Then Jean-Baptiste appears in his white navy uniform. Camille abruptly tears herself from the hands of her stepmother, who was just speaking some affectionate words to her. Camille wants to leap into the arms of Jean-Baptiste, but at the door she is held back by a fat man, a friend of Eliane's, an anti-Communist who has been caring for Camille as a father would. Eliane rushes out the door and has an argument with Jean-Baptiste. She gives him a melodious slap, which he returns.

The workers defiantly sit on the ground and do not move. The machines grind to a halt, everything is at a standstill. Eliane, distraught but just as resolute as the workers, enters the workshop and begins to operate the machine. An old man, her father no doubt, begins to knead the rubber mass and feed it into the machine. The workers are surprised at the unexpected reaction of their employers. They are moved, and this human warmth destroys their will to revolt. Hesitantly, they rise to their feet and return to their places in the workshop. The old order has been restored to its quotidian state. For the moment: Eliane's two human hands alone will not suffice to uphold the old colonial world order much longer.

"Independence? Yes, that's what people say nowadays. In reality, things look different. Independence is a trinket one gives a woman to make her happy." Jean's words reached my ears through the mouth of Ai Van. "What are you trying to say?" "For example, we give economic support to the former colonies in West Africa." "Support? The investors need someone who is dependent on them," I said to Ai Van while keeping my eyes fixed on Jean. "When we support others, we gain no profit from this." "Yes you do. Those who support others always get the sweetest juice to drink—juice with no brand name. Therefore, I can't be more specific." "You still have all that old propaganda in your head," Ai Van interrupted me, horrified. "It isn't propaganda, I saw it in a movie!" "But a movie is a work of fiction."

I wished I were able to vanquish Jean and Ai Van with incisive arguments. But I couldn't even speak properly. And my words lacked legitimacy, for I was sleeping in an apartment for which Jean paid the rent and eating from Ai Van's pots and dishes.

Yoko Tawada

•

Camille marches through the city alongside her French class-mates, all of them light-footed, singing and dressed in school uniforms. A procession of prisoners trudges in the opposite direction. Perhaps these are the men who tried to escape their work, or even were planning an uprising. In any case, it is foreseeable that their march will end in death. One of them breaks away and starts running. A Frenchman in uniform shoots and misses. The prisoner dashes into the midst of the schoolgirls, seizes the girl standing beside Camille, and holds her body in front of him as a shield. He is about to flee again when there is another gunshot. The prisoner is struck, blood spurts out of him, landing on Camille, who closes her eyes. There is a faint taste of blood on her lips. I know how it is with blood: He who drinks the blood of a snake that has been killed will later understand the language of birds and become a prophet. Camille is still an inexperi-enced, spoiled girl from the plantation, but the blood spat-tered on her lips will be her first taste of the Communism that will gradually spread throughout her body.

When Camille regains consciousness, she is a baby, bare-chested, lying on her back. A new mother wipes the sweat from her breast. Oddly, Camille's breasts are not the breasts of a baby but rather those of a pubescent girl. Her nipples harden with arousal, her sweat is red, and the mother is a man: Jean-Baptiste, who found her unconscious and rescued her.

Because she is so in love, Camille is paralyzed for days. She does not speak, and she secretly weeps in the garden pavilion. Eliane is worried; she asks her what's wrong. With naïve candor, Camille replies that she's in love. Eliane's face distorts with pity. Apparently, she is convinced that being in love must of necessity be a torment. Off-handedly she asks, "With whom?", knowing this to be a question of little importance as a girl's love is not dependent on the object of this love. Still, Camille's response slices Eliane's heart in two.

In an old fairy tale I knew, a stepmother gave her stepdaughter shoes made of stinging nettles. When the girl refused to put them on, her stepmother stuck a pin in her eye. This took place beside a spinning wheel. I couldn't quite remember how the story went. Perhaps the stepmother forced her stepdaughter to drink her blood from one shoe or sleep in a bed of cold cinders. I also had read a modern novel in which a mother fell in love with a man and for his sake left her own natural-born daughter. Eliane, though, wasn't a character in a fairy tale or modern novel. Her stepdaughter was a thorn that Eliane always wanted to keep at her side, even if it cost her an eye.

Eliane seems not to be struggling with Camille over Jean-Baptiste, only with Jean-Baptiste over Camille. Camille loves

Jean-Baptiste; for her, he is a substitute mother whom she is allowed to desire. Regardless of how much Camille loves Eliane and vice versa, they cannot remain together. Eliane could go on living with Camille and forget Jean-Baptiste. But Camille leaves Eliane's house. If Jean-Baptiste were now to return to Eliane, she wouldn't give him Camille's room.

An adoptive mother chooses a daughter for herself. This is not the same as a natural mother who becomes pregnant against her will and gives birth to the child because she wasn't able to abort it. With a natural mother, you can never be sure whether or not she wanted the child. Nor can you ever know if she truly wanted to have a daughter and not a son. This is why I always found the love of an adoptive mother more credible than anything else. My aunt once told me the story of Racine's *Phaedra*. The stepmother in this play was in love with her son, which was unacceptable in her social circle. Therefore she tormented her son so cruelly that he left home. Since then I have understood why stepmothers in fairy tales must always be unkind to their children.

"There also used to be a lot of love stories involving a princess and her stepmother, but unfortunately all these tales have been lost," my aunt said. Stepmothers like that must have been burned as witches along with their love stories.

•

This is a revolution of the family novel: Eliane is not jealous. She leaves her lover because she prefers her adopted daughter to him. Initially, I was quite certain that Eliane wasn't jealous of Camille. The fourth time I saw the movie, however, I felt slightly unsettled, for I saw that your beauty was a carefully prepared surface free of any expression. No straightforward message forced me into the narrow space of understanding. Particularly in close-ups your face was fascinatingly open, like a screen before the movie begins. It was my own illness that I always wanted to project a feeling onto it.

When the last name flew by and the music stopped, I noticed that the man sitting two seats over did not get up; he was observing me. Usually I didn't look the other moviegoers in the eye, but in this case I couldn't avoid it, for the man spoke to me while moving his hand across the back of the seat until it reached my shoulder. A Frenchman, roughly thirty years old, khaki-colored corduroys. His jacket was of the same material as his pants, his black hair was curly at the nape of his neck. I didn't understand him. He continued to make an effort, speaking ever clearer and louder, in shorter sentences. I recognized your name. He pointed at me and said, "Tristana." "No, I'm not Tristana," I replied. He shook his head and said, "Miriam." He seemed to have noticed that I only went to movies with you in them. Then he wrote down a sentence on a piece of paper, along with a time, a date, and the name of a movie theater and handed it to me. His sentence even contained a word I could understand: *rencontre*, meeting. He wanted to see me again.

Yet again I was in Indochina. I went to the movies almost every day. Like an alcoholic who has stopped counting the empty bottles, I stopped counting how many times I'd seen this film. I would have felt ashamed if I ran into that man before the appointed day. At the same time, I wished to see him again as soon as possible and looked for him cautiously each time I walked into the movie theater. Each time the auditorium contained only unfamiliar faces.

Sometimes the language of the film struck me as too primitive: a young man with neatly trimmed hair and glasses, for example, is an intellectual, uncompromising, and later will become a Communist and leave the house of his birth. Or his mother who wears an expensive silk blouse and never puts down her abacus is a good businesswoman and conservative. Or a worker, her husband, and her small children who flee the place where they have been exploited unendurably are good-natured. On the road they meet Camille, but sooner or later they are captured and bound to stakes near the shore so that the ocean will slowly drown them as the tide rises. When the water retreats, their pale corpse faces appear. Camille's shock is more than understandable. Only the face of Eliane never loses its ambiguity. It withdraws more and more from the violence of the images, providing a quiet refuge outside the film's plot to give my longing someplace to go.

Communist, anarchist, terrorist. I love these words because I can recognize them even in French. Camille is arrested as a Communist. Her life in the labor camp is not shown. One day the door of the camp is opened. I don't know how much time has elapsed since her arrest. Eliane hurries through the crowds of people—she's come to get Camille. Every person in the crowd is trying to find his liberated relatives or friends. In the throng, Eliane loses her elegant hat, then finally sees Camille, rushes up to embrace her and asks question after question, speaking to her so lovingly it's almost painful to hear. This is more affection than she's ever shown for any man, but Camille's gaze is hovering in midair, strangely unmoved. After a while she says the words that cause Eliane to burst into tears. Camille weeps, too. I'm glad I don't understand these words.

I was afraid to learn Camille's reply. At the same time, I couldn't get it out of my mind. I convinced Ai Van to come to the movies with me and translate this line. "Go back to France! Indochina no longer exists! It is dead!" my interpreter, Ai Van, whispered in my ear. Within me it is Eliane who is weeping, not Camille. The lights turned on in the movie theater and my cheeks were still wet. Ai Van dragged me to a little ice-cream parlor and asked: "Why are you crying? Wouldn't you rather eat an ice cream? Did you see Camille's eyes when she was released? They were so inhuman. I can't understand these Communists. But the film wasn't bad."

I was still going to the clinic three times a week. They no longer took blood from me; instead they smeared ointments on my skin and then peeled my skin off bit by bit.

One Friday I was informed that Dr. Lee was ill. In her place, a man in a light-blue lab coat entered. He divided my back into forty-nine little squares and tested various salves. I looked at my back in the mirror, twisting my neck unnaturally to look behind me. "Some products really do have to be tested on a delicate, civilized back. You can't just try everything on rats—they are far too quick to adapt, like the foolish masses," the man said in jest. My mouth reacted quickly and thoughtlessly like the muscular reflexes of a frog right after it's been killed: "And you fled the country in 1975 because you didn't want to have anything to do with the foolish masses?" The man's fingers froze. After a moment of silence, he asked in return: "And you? An illegal alien?" "What do you mean by illegal? Or are the experiments you're doing here legal by any chance?" "Why would you come to us if you have such suspicions? Why don't you find some other job that suits you better? Not long ago someone saw you on the street at night. Why don't you try streetwalking?" I put on my clothes and left the clinic.

What was I supposed to do? I shouldn't have reacted so strongly. What would Ai Van say? I went home. The air in the apartment felt strangely chalky. Jean was sitting slumped at the kitchen table. When he turned around, his face suddenly looked very old. "Where is Ai Van?" Instead of answering, he ran his fingers over a piece of plastic on the table. There were many other plastic parts lying there as well, in various shapes. A child would use them to build a small airplane or a military vessel. Jean's pupils were fixed and red. I should have said something right away, but I couldn't think of a single word. There was a faint, artificial smell of glue. Jean patted his trousers, extracted a few banknotes, and handed them to me like an old neighbor I once knew. This neighbor used to give children candy and in exchange asked incomprehensible things of them. I was astonished, for I had never before received money directly from Jean. He attempted a grandfatherly smile. In Ai Van's presence, he generally was in the habit of keeping his face under control, impassive as a cowboy's. Now his muscles had let go of the flesh. A ray of light falling through the kitchen window turned his hair silver.

Chapter Six

Drôle d'endroit
pour une rencontre

My feet kept walking in a single direction. I stopped
nowhere, not even in front of a movie theater that
beckoned to me with its twinkling placards. Soon
there were no more shop signs, only slumbering apartment
buildings, followed by little parks, warehouses, gray walls,
and vacant lots.

It was already dark by the time I reached the parking lot.

A single car was present, surrounded by the white lines separating the absent cars from one another. A public bathroom, a cigarette vending machine. Whenever a car drove past, I flinched. I would see the car's two eyes without being able to make out the eyes of the driver. A policeman cruising by would stop to interrogate me. I was a suspicious woman in a parking lot—no car, no bags, no companion. It occurred to me that it might be better to keep out of sight, so I walked toward the women's bathroom. Cold, moldy air rose from the sodden earth by the entrance. Midges hovered around a lantern like bits of fluff. They were remnants, left over from summer, or perhaps shrunken vampires, the afterimage of a film. Why was I here when I could be sitting in a movie theater? Was I planning to spend the night in this damp, cold bathroom? The money in my pocket was barely enough for a movie ticket, let alone a night in a hotel. I left the bathroom and immediately was attacked by a harsh light. I shielded my face with my elbows. There was a screech of brakes. The door of the car opened, and a rectangular businessman stepped out. "What are you doing here?" I couldn't have explained my situation even in my native tongue. The man demanded an instant response. With both hands he gripped my shoulders, shaking them violently while yelling: "What are you doing here? What happened? Say something! Speak!" I put my right hand in my pants pocket as if I had an explanation stored inside. My fingers were surprised by a slip of paper. I held it to the dim light of the lantern. The man tore the paper out of my hand and read it aloud in his gravelly voice. Then he roughly put a hand on my back, which was still sore from the skin experiments, and pushed me into his car. I remembered the young man who'd given me the note at the movie theater. The word "meeting," a date, a time, and the name of a cinema. With an exasperated expression, the man stepped on the gas and abruptly drove off. When we arrived at the theater, the young man came running up to me. When I turned back to look at the man in the car, he was already gone.

The young man asked me something, probably who the man in the car was. He could have been asking something quite different. "I don't know." My answer had to be doubly correct, for I knew neither what had been asked nor who this man was. The two of us dove shoulder to shoulder into the warm darkness of the movie theater and sat there like twins in the womb. I stared in astonishment at the title that appeared on the screen. The sentence with the word "meeting" the young man had written on the slip of paper he'd given me was the title of the film. So he hadn't in fact written that he wanted to see me again.

The woman being played by you is having an argument with a man in a car. We don't hear any voices, just the background noise of the highway. Where were we moviegoers sitting if we couldn't hear you? And where were you? Through the car's windshield the couple sees a white creature floating beside the road. It is a woman in fluttering pajamas. She throws herself in front of the car, and the squealing tires barely miss the body of the would-be suicide. The car drives on. The couple continue their argument. Soon the car slows and pulls off into a deserted parking lot. The door opens and the woman is thrown out of the car, followed by her fur coat. The car traces an elegant curve and vanishes into the night. The woman gets up calmly. At first the parking lot looks deserted, but this isn't true: a man stands beside a car with a raised hood. He approaches the woman, speaks to her in a bantering tone of voice, and then for some reason imitates a hen. The woman's gaze keeps hovering at an altitude where neither a hen nor this man can be found. The man returns to his car; he carefully inspects the parts of the engine while poring over an instruction manual. The woman wraps herself in her fur coat, shivering. The fur, blond hair, skin, high heels: together these things possess an aura that appears on the screen as tiny golden feathers. The feathers are inconspicuously growing in the damp night air. The man wears only a shirt and a thin jacket but doesn't seem to feel the cold. He retrieves some tennis socks and jogging shoes from the car and offers them to the woman. Her well-formed legs now have big clumps at the end. These humorous proportions call to mind an ostrich, but they render the beauty of the woman's face all the more striking. Nonetheless, there is something missing for me in this face that I admired in *Indochine.*

The next scene of the film: a highway rest stop. The car and its disassembled engine parts have been moved, at the insistence of the traffic cops, in front of the rest stop building. The man and woman are sitting together at a table. The dining room has a lightness made of plastic.

The man can't make up his mind. He leaves the table, walks over to the engine parts, returns. After a while, he leaves the table again. Later the woman leaves the rest stop, gets into the car and speaks to the man. She begins to kiss him absent-mindedly, as if possessed, as if she were trying to kiss all the microscopic angels floating in the air. Her nerves are charmingly frazzled, but her madness is not as anarchical as in *Repulsion*—there is something sentimental about it. Didn't you go much farther in London when you were scarcely more than a girl? Have you forgotten your repulsion? In this film you are a woman who has been abandoned and is waiting for something to happen. You are a middle-class woman who is sensitive and sweet and coincidentally happens to find herself in crisis. This crisis is boring. Why don't you bite the neck of the drowsy man to drink his fresh blood? In New York you'd have lost no time doing so. Now here you are sitting around groaning in a little French suburb. This man, lethargic as he appears, might one day, under different circumstances, be wide awake and courageous enough to take part in the resistance movement against the National Socialists. Then you as his beloved would surely play a quite different role, for example, the role of a stage actress whose Jewish husband, the owner of the theater, is hiding in the basement. You have only four years left before you'll be confronted with the revolution in Indochina. Are you ready? What revolution are you waiting for at this highway rest stop?

After the curtain closed, the young man brought me to an ice-cream parlor. I asked his name. "Charles," he replied, and we both laughed, since the hero of the film was also called Charles. "And what is your name?" I gave myself the name "Thu Huong," which I had never before used, and translated it for him as "perfume of autumn."

Autumn was beginning to scatter its leaves. Through the window I saw trampled leaves lying like shadows on the sidewalk. After Charles ordered two coffees for us, he started explaining something I was unable to comprehend. I would have given up quickly if he hadn't kept repeating his sentences so tenaciously. It had to do with names. When you heard a name, the thing being named was suddenly far away. He was saying something like this, though I wasn't sure whether these were his own thoughts on my name, or the words of Charles in the movie. Your name in this film was "France." How extraordinary that a person and her country could share a name.

Charles took a sip of coffee and said he had to make

a quick phone call. As soon as he disappeared in the basement, I began to worry. What should I say if he wanted to
escort me home afterward? What would I do if he didn't
try to escort me home and just left me alone on the street?
If he invited me to his home, I would follow him at once
and never leave him.

Charles returned and gave me a nod. Someone would
be coming, a friend of his who had something to do with
Vietnam. The foamed milk on top of the coffee was unusually thick and firm. Soon a young, Vietnamese-looking man
appeared and greeted Charles like an old friend. He looked
a little like Camille's fiancé in *Indochine*. Charles introduced
him, saying, "This is my friend Tuong Linh."

Tuong Linh was a surgeon. He had emigrated to Paris
with his family as a twelve-year-old, and later had studied
medicine here. When Charles was brought to the hospital
after a motorcycle accident, Tuong Linh was the doctor who
had operated on his broken chin. Then they became friends.
"Usually I avoid making friends with a patient. Charles
was an exception, because he was a impossible patient. One
day after the operation he escaped from the hospital and
went to the movies. By coincidence, I was there, too. Before
the film started, I noticed a head two rows in front of me
that was braced with plaster and wrapped in a bandage.
The head turned to the side, and I realized it had been
lying beneath my knife only twenty hours before." Charles
was smirking. "But you didn't come talk to me right away

because you wanted to see the film. An egotistical doctor!" "What film was it?" "*Un flic.*" Tuong Linh looked at me and asked if I, too, was a passionate moviegoer. I immediately said "no," regretted it at once and looked down because my cheeks were burning. They wouldn't believe me if I said there wasn't any other place I could survive except on the screen with you and that this was the only reason why I watched films. I couldn't tell Tuong Linh about my cinema compulsion, my film fever. I always thought it was because I couldn't speak that I couldn't explain things. This excuse no longer counted since I could have explained everything to Tuong Linh in Vietnamese. I was as mute as I was in French. I could feel my heart pounding, and my throat was scratchy despite the soothing foamy milk. Tuong Linh didn't push me, nor did he look disappointed. He spoke with Charles for a while about something else, then turned to me again and asked where I lived. "I don't live anywhere any more. For various reasons I no longer have a home." Tuong Linh took me home with him without posing any more questions.

His apartment was unusually spacious for a single person. Pictures were hanging on the walls, among them a painting that showed a flat landscape with a large amount of sky. A Chinese ink painting depicted an emaciated hermit in the mountains. The bookshelf was completely filled with books that bore French titles on their mostly crêpe-yellow spines. It had been years since I'd read any literature.

Back when I still went to school, I'd been addicted to books. Sometimes I even read when I was walking on the street and would trip over the baskets of the women selling vegetables. Suddenly I was seized by the burning desire to devour every single one of Tuong Linh's books.

Tuong Linh was a calm and quiet man. The next morning he gave me a set of keys and told me to rest.

I liked the overpowering scent emanating from Tuong Linh's fingers. It reminded me of the way a certain soap smelled. I no longer remembered where I had washed my hands with this soap.

"I'm so happy I met you. Though I have once more missed my chance to learn French. I can go on living without speaking with anyone except you." "Don't you want to learn French?" "Yes, very much. But …"

On the first evening, Tuong Linh gave me the only pillow he owned. Under his own head he placed his white sweater, neatly folded up.

"You've gone out with Charles many times now, so you must speak French." "The language of our dates is the movie schedule—a language that cannot be misunderstood. I can't say anything else to him." "Do you like him?" "Yes, very much."

When Tuong Linh had a day off, Charles would visit us and make us duck with white beans and other tasty dishes.

His eyes and fingers flew ceaselessly back and forth between cutting board, knife, faucet, and the pot on the stove, while his mouth didn't stop providing me new information about you. He liked to read film magazines and knew, for example, that you had two children of your own, what they were called, and who their fathers were. I wasn't so interested in your private life as this private person was a stranger to me. What I wanted to know was what exactly Eliane had thought about Communism, and what Carol did for a living after she had regained consciousness. I also wanted to know when the next movie you were in was coming out. "You don't have to keep us entertained at the same time as you're cooking for us," Tuong Linh said, but Charles ignored him and went on talking.

Tuong Ling returned from work each day with his head numb, deadened, stuffed full. It wasn't possible for him to catch a second wind in the evening and go out to the movies. So I would go alone, or else with Charles. Every time we went to a movie together, he would take me out for coffee afterward and would tirelessly ask me questions that I didn't understand right away. He wouldn't give up until I'd answered them. Sometimes he was completely satisfied with my reply even though I hadn't understood his question and had just blurted something out. Perhaps not understanding or misunderstanding a question is something that often happens even to other people. No one notices, though, since the answers one gives generally happen to fit the questions anyhow.

When he finished his coffee, Charles would always ask me what time it was, although he knew I didn't have a watch on either. I understood this question right away when someone asked it in a movie. It was a strange feeling to understand a question right away. The question leapt into my brain cells so quickly I had no time to feel the question's body. What time is it now? France asks this of the man who appears utterly uninterested in the time but nevertheless owns a watch. The man freezes there for two seconds as if he first must make sense of something unexpected.

I knew from Tuong Linh that Charles had quit his studies and was working at a gas station. "It's not a bad job, as you can see," Charles said to me as we were watching the film *Les parapluies de Cherbourg* together. In this film, the climax of a drama took place at a gas station. "Then again the woman didn't wait for her lover; she married a rich man instead," Charles added, sighing.

Tuong Linh loved the composer Richard Strauss. I had never heard of him. When Tuong Linh came home, the first thing he would do was turn on the stereo. A floating soprano voice stroked his pale cheeks coldly, gently. I was afraid of this voice that was trying to carry Tuong Linh off into a gravity-free zone like a whirlwind. He poured red wine into a glass and drank down his own silence. I felt guilty, since there was nothing I could do to give him his strength back. "You should just think of yourself until you are free of your shackles," he said to me. I didn't know where he got the idea of shackles as I hadn't told him anything about myself.

Later I began to study Tuong Linh's CD covers when he was out. *Vier letzte Lieder* was printed on one of them. Why *letzte*? I recognized this German word and remembered that it had once elicited a mild feeling of hunger in me.

In the kitchen cupboard I found perfectly stacked packages of glass noodles, shark fins, morels, shiitake mushrooms and rice paper, as well as lotus roots and oyster sauce. I carefully removed the morels and lotus roots from their packages and looked at them for a long time as though I'd never seen them before.

I began to cook this and that. It went surprisingly well, though in the end I wasn't sure whether a particular sauce hadn't once tasted fishier and less salty, whether the consistency of the cooked glass noodles and morels shouldn't be more yielding or firmer. "I can't eat anything in the evening anyway," Tuong Linh said and didn't touch the food.

Once, when he was out, I tried calling Ai Van. In the background the song *Im Abendrot* was playing at full volume. I had meanwhile discovered that this was the piece the Charles in the movie put on and then asked France if she liked it. She didn't respond. In his broken-down car, the stereo system was the only thing still working.

I had already prepared my life story for Ai Van. It lay there on its platter, waiting to be served: "At the movies I happened to run into an old friend. She lives in the South of France, where her husband owns a vineyard. She said she could offer me a job there and drove me right away so I wouldn't have to pay train fare. I'll come back to Paris when I've saved enough money." I let the telephone ring ten times, Ai Van seemed not to be home. I left a message on the answering machine saying I would get back in touch when I had a permanent address in the South of France.

One day I made a date to meet Charles at eight p.m. at a movie theater. We were seeing the same film again. He never used to see a movie more than once, but now my repetition compulsion had infected him. When I got home, Tuong Linh wasn't sitting on his sofa as usual; he was at the dining table, eating. Several bowls of food I had cooked for myself during the day were spread out on the table. He gave me a brochure for a language school and asked if I would marry him. During the night the thought occurred to me that there was perhaps a great misunderstanding between us. But I didn't know where the place was where I could correct the error.

When I woke up, I was alone in the apartment. Tuong Linh had the early shift. I spent the whole day looking through the film magazines Charles had given me. In the evening Tuong Linh came home earlier than usual and asked me first thing if I had looked through the language school pamphlets. "No, not yet." "But you've got to do something for yourself, otherwise you'll remain a hopeless young girl forever. I don't want a young girl. I want to marry you." "That isn't possible." "Why not?" "Because I don't have a visa." "A person isn't born with a visa like a talent. The visa has to be arranged for after the fact. I have a friend who is a lawyer. He will help us." "Not every lawyer is willing to help his friend." "I know. But this one will help us."

If I had a visa, I could learn the language and study at the university. It wasn't too late yet to catch up with my peers. Plus it wasn't as if I'd been loafing all these years while the others were going to school. I was studying a science that had no name. I was studying it on the screen, along with you.

Chapter Seven

Belle de Jour

Hopeful as little bells ringing, ominous as clanking chains, a sound is approaching in 2/4 time. The coachman and his colleague sit side by side wearing black top hats and tailcoats that remind me of bats. Behind them sits a young woman who is being played by you. Beside her sits a man of about thirty, possibly the son of a large landowner. His prosperity strikes him as a natural talent. I used to flippantly describe such men as pigs from the upper classes. In this man's face, however, one could discern both seriousness of purpose and a sense of responsibility—qualities I'd only ever seen in the faces of a very few, young Party members. The man and the woman speak together intimately; then a shadow passes over the eyes of the woman and the face of the man turns stony. He stops the carriage, forces the woman to get out. She refuses, and he orders the bats to help him. They pull the woman out of the carriage, grab her by the wrists, and drag her body through the woods like a sack of grain.

Secretly I was watching Charles, who was sitting beside me. The expression on his face was blank. When the screen brightened after the next change of scene, reflections from the screen flickered on his eyebrows. He didn't notice I was watching him.

From a thick branch hangs a rope with which the woman's wrists are bound. The man tears her dress, baring her back, and commands the bats to give her a whipping. The woman moans, rejoicing at this punishment. What does it mean to play a role? After all it is you doing the moaning and no other woman. Have you submitted to being whipped because you regretted having whipped a worker in Indochina? It wasn't your fault that Eliane was born into the ruling class that exploits others. Why wasn't the son of the landowner having himself whipped instead of his wife? The whip slices the wind into tatters, the woman screams—it is surely painful, and yet there is no real tension. The participants are bathing together in lukewarm violence.

The son of the landowner gives the younger of the two bats a sign. This bat walks up to the woman and nibbles the back of her neck. She moans; he looks coarse and uneducated. Typical for the culture before the Revolution, I think. In the previous century, aristocratic families gave their painters a lot of money to make them appear more beautiful in their paintings.

The man who is having his wife whipped appears two hundred years later as an upright citizen in pressed pajamas. He has the same woman with him, also dressed in pajamas. The two of them are having a relaxed conversation as if there had never been an act of violence between them. The man speaks gently, almost politely to the woman. Did this man replace his heart with another one when he was reborn, or does this scene mean that one and the same man can act differently under different social circumstances?

The cruel, upright husband and his black-haired friend are standing in a field, stirring a light-gray mass in a bucket with shovels. It is a mixture of muddy earth and cow dung. While the horses move with regular steps along the broad avenue, the cows are anarchistically scattered in the landscape. The woman is dressed in breezy white garments like a Korean shaman, but once more she is tied up and suffering like a Catholic saint. The men throw handfuls of dung at her chest, belly, and face.

I don't know how this cow dung episode can be integrated into her bourgeois existence. The different times are playing cards that are constantly being reshuffled in memory and then laid blindly upon the table. No fixed order defines the relationships between the cards. The pips remain hidden until the cards are flipped over. My last day of school in Ho Chi Minh City and the boring math class on the inscrutable topic "differential equations" I fell asleep in had no connection with the moment my airplane landed at Schönefeld Airport. The hour at the hotel restaurant in East Berlin was cut off from the hours in the pizzeria in Bochum with its glittering slot machines. And the seeds from the rapeseed fields of Bochum couldn't drift all the way to Paris. I could no longer trace the points in time leading back to Saigon since these points were now scattered across the Earth.

This director was not gentle with you. In another film he cut off one of your legs, and this time he has you whipped and pelted with cow dung. "He also made a film about the Revolution, but I think he was more Catholic than Communist," Charles said.

After the movie I walked home alone. Charles said he had a date, and I suppressed my urge to ask with whom. As we said goodbye, he asked succinctly, "When will you be marrying Tuong Linh?" "Soon." "It's good that you met him." "Thank you. That was a gift from you." "It was your destiny." His soft curls bore the faint scent of cigarettes I didn't recognize.

Sometimes on my way to the theater I would observe people as if they were part of some movie I knew. The men sitting beneath the awning of a café, peacefully drinking espresso: perhaps they too had their wives whipped in another scene. If only I could rewind the film to learn all these things! I saw women standing at the edge of the sidewalk. With longing in their eyes, they watched for an empty taxi. The paper bags they were carrying contained not the clothing they'd just bought at a boutique but whips.

On my way back from the theater, I would retrace the series of images I'd seen in the movie. If I yanked the strip of film from the projector and used it to make my own road, I could walk down it image by image all the way home.

The woman you are playing is named Séverine. She sits in the back of a taxi. Her friend next to her is excitedly talking. There is something solidly bumpkin-like about her young face, and her head resembles a chestnut. Despite the great agitation in her voice, there is nothing about her that suggests she might be on the verge of a breakdown. She would rather send other women to walk the streets than so much as peer down an alleyway herself. Séverine is amused by her friend's report, but soon a plan appears in her eyes. Cut.

Séverine is walking through the city, which is reposing in daylight. A sign says "CITE Jean de Saumur." Séverine nervously inspects her surroundings. A young woman with painstakingly made-up eyes and erotically disheveled hair walks past, casting an observant, somewhat envious glance at this beautiful sister-woman, and vanishes into the building at number eleven. Séverine leaves the square, cools her heels for a while in a park, and then returns to the same place. This time she slips stealthily into the building and rings at the door marked "Anaïs." A short-haired young woman, slender and severe, opens the door. In her polished gemstone eyes, Séverine probably looks like a girl in need of help. The young woman scrutinizes the applicant thoroughly. She is apparently in charge of this establishment. Should money be invested in this product? Her cool-headed gaze contains a trace of that feverish consumerism that might overcome another woman at a boutique. The boss decides to keep Séverine and kisses her on the lips. Séverine tries to avert her lips from those of her employer but she is too late. Two seconds of lip paralysis pass, and the kiss seals the contract.

There are already two cheerful women working for the boss in this apartment. When they gather at a table in the living room, the atmosphere changes to that of a girls' school. A well-dressed customer rings the bell and enters the apartment. A short man with hair like strands of cotton-wool—a Martian. The women surround him, trying to catch his fancy. The man uncorks a bottle of champagne, hands the women a magic box as a gift, and laughs like a broken washing machine. From his Martian face gleam the eyes of a brutal child. Séverine stands alone in a corner, her back to the others. The Martian points to her. He has chosen her as his purchase for the day. The boss orders her new employee to go to the bedroom with the man. Séverine refuses, but is secretly pleased when the boss with the severe gaze and harsh words gives her a little shove from behind. The zipper of her dress is opened. To my surprise, your limbs, chest, and belly are as toned as those of a champion swimmer. Your body now covered only by marble-smooth undergarments displays no superfluous flesh, no fat, no milky softness. The man throws Séverine on the bed. Cut.

With the other movie, which was set in the parking lot and at the highway rest stop, I felt I was seeing all the events of the story. There were no sudden cuts. But in this film the scenes that might have been provocative and interesting always ended abruptly in fade-outs, as in *Tristana*. Who was doing that, and why? I didn't have to be made any more curious than I already was. My eyes wanted to see everything.

And what happened to the pictures that were cut out of the film?

At first you didn't reveal to me that your name is Séverine—you call yourself "Beauty of the Day." In the same building in which strange men are received lives a little girl whose name is also Séverine. A workman caresses her body, the priest shoves wafers made of sperm into her mouth, and several women praise her for her good grades at school. Séverine just stands there silently, her back ramrod straight.

I didn't know how one referred to a parlor in which women played cards while waiting for strange men. I caught the word "maison" and then something else that sounded like "publique." My idea of a house open to the public would be, say, a museum or a library. In school I learned that a capitalist society was just a huge bordello. Therefore it was quite natural for a woman who worked in a bordello to be an integral part of this society.

    Séverine returns home, where her husband is waiting. During the day he wears a lab coat, and in the evenings he sits at his desk studying medical journals. Séverine sits on the opposite side of the desk wearing a pink nightgown. They sleep in separate beds that are arranged side by side. Between them is a gap of perhaps fifty centimeters. This distance is not large, but it is unbridgeable. One time the man tries to creep into Séverine's bed. She makes a slight gesture of refusal, and at once he desists.

Séverine enjoys submitting to the power of her procuress, who is far more severe than her customers. During daytime hours, "Beauty of the Day" belongs to her. Mao said that each person should work according to his abilities and take what he truly needs. Séverine is not merely a worker, she is also a product. She wishes to become a thing, complete with chest, thighs, neck, and buttocks: this is her own desire, her own decision as a worker. What would Mao say about this?

A Mongolian beekeeper comes to the bordello. I'm not sure if he's really Mongolian, but the actor's name is Genghis Kahn or something like that. Despite his enormous body, he looks kind, but the women in the bordello are afraid of him. In a small black-lacquered box he is holding something that is buzzing. Surely a bee, perhaps even an electrical one, for the buzzing sounds artificial. One of Séverine's colleagues peeks into the box and exclaims in horror: "Non!" Séverine, though, embraces the beekeeper and beams, which is something she never does. The procuress is watching Séverine's reaction with astonishment. With this customer she would have been prepared, for once, to accept a refusal. The beekeeper accompanies Séverine into the back room, and shows her with his chin, eyes, and voice that she should keep her brassiere on. She is to bare only the lower part of her body. The combination of milk and honey produces weariness so most beekeepers are afraid of milk and the body part from which it flows. The Mongolian beekeeper takes a tiny little bell from his pocket and rings it. Perhaps a ceremony to drive out evil spirits. Séverine laughs unabashedly. The film doesn't show us what happens between the two of them after Séverine has surrendered the lower half of her body to the bees.

The beekeeper is gone. I'm not sure he really was a beekeeper. Séverine remains on her belly for a long time, buried in her thick hair. Finally she lifts her face, which is radiant.

If you happen to have a weakness for Mongolian beekeepers, it's possible you might like me. The landscape of my face is a mixture between the Indochinese peninsula and the Mongolian steppe. My mother once told me there was a Mongolian among our ancestors. He rode from the steppe all the way to our seaside home to pay obeisance to the Emperor and bring him honey. On the very day he arrived at the palace, he fell in love with a court lady who sat in a boat on the pond, singing wondrous melodies. He leapt into the water to reach her. As a Mongolian he was good with horses but had no clue about the properties of water. And so he flailed about in vain and soon sank beneath the water. The court lady undressed with lightning speed and leapt into the water to rescue the beekeeper. She pulled him out, laid him on the grass, and tended to him for three days and three nights. Later she gave birth to my grandfather's grandfather. Perhaps this, too, was a story without roots and leaves, for my mother often made up stories. But I didn't care whether it was a lie or not—my face had certain Mongolian traits. Some day I'll visit you, I'll knock at the door of your house and say that I'm the beekeeper's daughter. You'll open the door and let me in.

The considerate husband in pressed pajamas has no idea what his wife likes to do during daylight hours. I knew you better than he did. I'd already made your acquaintance in *Repulsion*. At the time you were only twenty-two. I also knew you as a twenty-one-year-old in *Les parapluies de Cherbourg*. Séverine's husband had no way of knowing these segments of your life, for he was only a character in a movie. He wasn't permitted to see another film.

I was alone when I saw this film for the second time. I had called Charles three times that evening, but he wasn't home. Tuong Linh sat down on the sofa and asked me how the movie was. Often he tried to relax by listening to me rather than talking about his work. Even on Sundays when the alarm clock didn't ring at six, he got up by seven at the latest, quickly made himself a pot of green tea, and sat down at his desk. "Are there any new movies?" he would ask. He still didn't have the strength to go to the movies in his free time and saw me as his deputy. I was permitted—even expected—to go to the movies in his place. "It's fun to go to the movies with Charles," he would say, even though it was I and not he who was the one going to the movies with Charles. "Charles hasn't been home much lately." "Perhaps he's been struck by Cupid's arrow. It would certainly be a shame for such a wonderful man to be alone forever," Tuong Linh said, laughing. I realized I was jealous.

You can't look into other people's heads, a thought that often occurred to me when I strolled down the Boulevard Saint-Michel. In the anonymity of daylight, I was gradually losing my fear of wandering around the city. Earlier I'd avoided large, bustling, festooned streets like the Boulevard St. Germain. Now it frightened me more to walk down a tiny street, the rue Serpente for example. Someone might peer into my head, for instance when I stopped in the used bookshop where you could buy cheap back-issues of film magazines. Several times already I'd entered this shop and sat down on the floor beside the low bookshelf to examine one magazine after another, flipping through them as if obsessed, feverishly pursuing your image.

Between emerging from the métro and disappearing again into the darkness of a movie theater, I would see women whose real-life roles I was unable to determine. They made a point of giving off an air of eroticism, for the very possibility of appearing prudish would have been enough to render them suspect, even antisocial. The length of their skirts was chosen with diplomatic precision: two centimeters longer than might count as indecent, and two centimeters too short to risk the stigma of prudishness. When the evening sun chanced to shine down on a round, white table in a café, turning it into a dazzling mirror, even one of these upstanding bourgeois ladies might get swallowed up by the mirror, never to return. In this looking-glass world, such a lady might eat pears with legs and hairy skin, gigantic Adam's apples and calluses on their heels. In return, she would receive payment from her customers in a currency that no longer existed. While the bill was being settled, her labia would flush as red as the flag that used to stand on the podium during Party meetings. Neither her husband nor her lover would have the slightest idea.

What would Tuong Linh say if he saw the images being projected in the cinema in my head? Sometimes he gave me a worried look, the unasked question trembling on his lips. I would stand behind him and place my hands on his shoulders the same way I had seen you do. Tuong Linh would lean back a little and ask me if I had studied the pamphlets from the language school. "No, not yet." "Why not? You've got to take some action yourself. I'd gladly do everything for you, but first of all I don't have the time, and secondly it's better for a person to take responsibility for his own life."

He would then take my hands, which were still lying on his shoulders, and remove them.

The next day I read through the information from the language school with the help of my dictionary. There was a beginners course listed that started four times a year. A form was attached that one could fill out to apply for the next course. I wrote down the name "Thu Huong" and felt as if I was doing this for some other person.

A woman who resembled Séverine's friend worked at the reception desk of the language school. She picked up my form, gave me a friendly smile, and said she needed to see my passport. I gasped. My passport was still in the pouch hanging around my neck, but anyone who looked at it could see I didn't have a visa. Plus it contained my real name. "Oh, I forgot my passport at home!" I quickly left the building. "No problem, just bring it with you when you come back!" the woman called after me.

In the evening I told Tuong Linh what had occurred. "We have to get you a visa. Until we do, you can't even go to school."

Chapter Eight

Si c'était à refaire

One Wednesday Tuong Linh came home early, at seven. "I have to talk to you." Outside a dog was howling. Tuong Linh's tongue quickly twirled about, though the individual syllables issuing from his lips remained upright and stiff. "At first I had the idea I would marry you in Vietnam and then return to Paris. As my spouse, you could enter France legally and remain here. Returning to Vietnam, however, could prove difficult for me, even if it were only for a wedding. As you know, my family left the country under complicated circumstances. I'd like to avoid even the slightest danger. Therefore, I thought of Thailand. What would you think of having a wedding in Thailand and returning to Paris with a marriage certificate?" "But when we leave France they'd check my passport and see I've been living here without a visa." "Yes, that's the problem," Tuong Linh sighed. "I don't want to violate any laws, though sometimes the law strikes me as such a heap of nonsense. I'm not planning to do anything harmful to mankind in any way. On the contrary. And nonetheless my actions would be punishable by law. The people who thought up these statutes were surely not thinking about us. And so we're not going to think about them either."

There was a Japanese painter known as "Heron" among his circle of acquaintances. Tuong Linh wasn't a close friend of his, but they'd known each other a long time. His real name was "Hiroo." I wasn't sure if this was his first or last name. Everyone just called him "Heron." He occasionally sold Japanese passports to people who needed them. Tuong Linh had a miniature Heron had painted hanging in his bathroom. Heron didn't sell many paintings, so he couldn't live off his art. Therefore he sometimes approached tourists to sell his pictures. When this didn't work, he would find people cheap places to stay on the outskirts of town. Heron would accompany the people there, and on the way he would skillfully remove their passports from their pockets and then sell them. Tuong Linh warned Heron not to keep pursuing this passport business, but Heron only shrugged and replied: "Yeah, I know. I'll be stopping soon anyway. A new time is coming in which passports will no longer have any value. Then I'll get into the internet business." Heron had studied art for years, but was unable to find a gallery interested in him, so he had no patrons. Nor could he find a rich woman to support him. A Japanese restaurant where he worked for a time fired him after he dropped his glasses into the hot oil sizzling with tempura. The plastic frames melted, a poisonous cloud rose from the pan, filling first the kitchen and then the entire restaurant. When I asked Tuong Linh jokingly if Heron was a member of a band of yakuza, he laughed and replied: "No. Perhaps most of the Japanese people in films are yakuza or samurai. Heron is an ordinary painter—he has ten fingers on each hand."

And so I could use the passport of a Japanese woman that Heron would be glad to sell me to leave France without a visa and travel to Thailand. There I could marry Tuong Linh and return to France as his wife with my own passport. Tuong Linh was satisfied with this plan. "What does such a passport cost?" I asked. "Don't worry. Your entire life depends on it, so how could it possibly be too expensive?"

•

It was the first time I'd ever been to Charles de Gaulle Airport. This place would bring me luck, for I'd heard that President Charles de Gaulle had spoken out against the use of force during the Vietnam War.

I myself never made Heron's acquaintance. Tuong Linh said I was better off not knowing much about him. Two weeks later Tuong Linh came home with a red Japanese passport on which a chrysanthemum bloomed. I'd heard that the Japanese make a tempura out of chrysanthemum blossoms that has a delicate, bitter flavor. I needed to learn by heart the name in the passport. It was both written in Chinese ideograms and transliterated. It made me nervous that I couldn't read the ideograms. If I'd been born before colonization, I would have been able to read them. Then I also could have been able to read Confucius in the original. Ho Chi Minh was not opposed to the introduction of the apparently simpler alphabetical writing system as he thought it preferable to illiteracy. Though I did wonder why there were fewer illiterates in China than in various other countries in which the alphabet was used.

On one of Tuong Linh's days off, we went to the Galeries Lafayette together to buy me a dress, a pair of shoes, and a handbag. "All right, now listen," Tuong Linh explained, "the main thing to look for is the brand names. It has to be obvious where the things come from." "Which brands are desirable?" "This one, for example, with the fat, crooked letters. This is the distorted monogram of a fashion designer." I picked out a light blue dress with a colorful collar and a gold chain-shaped belt and tried on both of them in the fitting room. Tuong Linh nodded and said to my reflection: "You look like a Japanese woman." I looked uneasily at my reflection, trying to ascertain whether my eyes were now sparking with capitalist consumer desires.

At the airport there was an artificial silence as if I were in a hospital ward before a major operation. Once, I had been operated on as a child. An old land mine had exploded near me on a school outing in the countryside. I was so shocked by the noise that for a while I didn't feel any pain. Only later did I see a piece of metal glittering in my thigh. I was brought to the hospital. I wasn't afraid of the operation, though I felt sick to my stomach. This is exactly the way I felt on the day of our flight to Thailand. I saw the checkpoint for passports in front of me, ran into the bathroom, and threw up. At the sink, a red-headed woman was changing her baby's diaper. She didn't even look at me, although she must have heard my retching from the bathroom stall. Perhaps vomiting was nothing special for her. Tuong Linh wasn't with me as we'd decided to go to the airport separately. He was a Vietnamese man with a French passport, while I was supposed to be a Japanese tourist. We had arranged to meet at the official taxi stand in front of the Bangkok airport.

In each glass box sat a man in uniform. The line I was

standing in shrank more rapidly than the others. It was my turn. A blond, uniformed man looked at my passport and chortled in Japanese "Kon-nichiwa!" I tried to remain calm. Surely this was the only Japanese sentence he knew. My supposition was correct, for he flipped through the passport and asked me in English how long I had been in France. "Ten days," I said in French. He exclaimed playfully, "Oh, how splendid, you speak French!" "No," I replied dully. Then he took a list out of a folder and glanced at it without interest. "What is your name, please?" he asked, his voice deeper. "Megumi Yamada," I replied fluently, as I had practiced often enough. The man picked up the telephone receiver, pressed a button, and started to speak with someone in a low voice. Tuong Linh had already warned me about this phone call. "Sometimes they act as if they are calling headquarters with this ridiculous plastic telephone in order to glean some crucial piece of information. I think the thing is just a prop. Or else they're ordering coffee for their break. Just don't make any unnecessary remarks about this. During a passport check in Moscow, a friend of mine once said to the man in uniform who was talking a long time on the phone, 'My greetings to the gentlemen in the Kremlin!' He got into a lot of trouble, and they searched him thoroughly, down to his earholes." The telephone call was lasting a long time. There was no more spit left in my mouth. When I coughed, two uniformed women appeared out of nowhere and gestured for me to go with them.

We walked down an endless corridor. Above our heads was a series of meaningless signs, arrows and letters, among other things the images of a little man and a little woman. I would never have suspected that in the middle of the crowded airport there could be a deserted corridor with numbered doors. We entered a room with a gray metal table and four folding chairs. The view from the window was a gray expanse. I didn't know if it was the wall of the next building or the sky. One of the women sat down across from me and the other beside me. "Do you speak French?" "No. Yes. No. Yes, a little." "Is this your passport?" "Yes." "Do you know a Japanese man named Hiroo?" "No." A few questions followed that I didn't understand. I could have said I didn't understand them. The two women were speaking to me politely as if I were their customer. In capitalism perhaps every person is a customer, even a prisoner. Then the women left the room to get something. I didn't even have the strength to get out of my chair to see if the door was locked. Tuong Linh surely must have noticed my absence at the gate by now, and had boarded the airplane alone.

The women returned with a man who was apparently Japanese. He was constantly wiping drops of sweat from his forehead although the air in the room was chilly. On his handkerchief I saw the brand name Tuong Linh had showed me at the department store. The Japanese man asked me questions in Japanese. I didn't respond. I quietly started to sob. Soon the Japanese man fell silent, too, and looked away. He was probably an ordinary businessman, perhaps a neighbor of one of the uniformed women.

I was taken somewhere by car and locked up in an attractive room. Ai Van and Jean had once suggested I play the role of a woman who's lost her memory in a car crash. It wasn't a bad idea. In any case it seemed easier to me to feign memory loss than to act out some other identity. I decided to shut myself away in the cell of oblivion and bar the door from within. My Vietnamese passport was in my suitcase, which I'd checked in. I hoped Tuong Linh would collect it from the conveyor belt in Bangkok and take it with him along with his own.

I tried to erase all the names I knew from my memory. "Tuong Linh" above all, then "Hiroo," who was apparently now a wanted man. The name "Ai Van" was even more dangerous, for she knew much more about me than the others. "Jean" was a common name which therefore meant next to nothing, and "Charles" was also a name shared by many men, including de Gaulle, my guardian spirit, who hadn't watched over me after all. The names of my family members were buried so deep inside me that I first had to dig them up to be able to erase them. Every morning I would recheck the list of names in my head and cross out any that had risen from my dreams to join the list.

•

The nausea didn't stop choking my consciousness. Apparently this feigned loss of memory was putting a strain on my stomach. When food tasted like ketchup or mayonnaise, I vomited on the spot. I no longer trusted things I had to swallow. I would have simply liked plain boiled potatoes on my plate. Whenever I chewed, I heard a grating voice in my temples: "You'll feel better if you vomit everything up again." "You don't have to swallow these bitter things alone. We share everything." "The truth is always smeared with ketchup. Lick it up!"

Who were these people who were trying to squeeze me out like a tube? Their weapons were hypnotism and drugs. One man who visited me every day seemed warm despite his lab coat, whereas the ones who had probably been sent by the police made me shiver. Their fingers, pale beneath the neon lights, were constantly taking notes when I wasn't speaking. Sometimes they shouted at me. I couldn't understand their language and would reply simply, "Correspondance! Correspondance!" repeating a word I'd found at the airport. It was difficult to remain silent when they spoke to me so loudly and roughly. I wanted to speak, but not like them. Otherwise I'd have made myself vulnerable to attack. Eventually the word "correspondance" was beaten to death, and I started saying "Déclaration! Déclaration!" This, too, was a word I'd found at the airport. I armed myself with these found words, for the words that belonged to me were too fragile. Life before the airport no longer existed for me. My first and only words came from the place from which I hadn't been able to fly.

In my imagination, I walked another twenty or thirty times down that airport corridor, accompanied by the two women. What had I done wrong? Why had they suddenly found me after leaving me in peace for eight years? I looked around as if I was trying to impress the last jewels of the free world on my memory. "Bureau for Found Objects" was printed on one door. How I would have loved to go into that room. Instead, we went into a room with a number on the door.

Two Vietnamese people were sent to talk to me. At first I trembled, but to my surprise their words didn't touch me at all. I could turn a deaf ear to the Vietnamese sentences as if they were a distant lullaby whose meaning was known to me but which no longer had access to my feelings.

Much more dangerous were the questions thrown at me by the man in the white lab coat. He would wait for a moment if I was distracted by some sound. Then he would quickly ask a question as if pouring water into the ear of a sleeping person. "Yesterday you were half asleep and mentioned an important name. Do you know who it was?" Caught off guard, I tried my best not to look startled, but he'd already seen my agitation. "Don't worry. This name is of no use whatsoever to the police, but to me it's helpful. Surprisingly, it was neither your own name nor the name of one of your friends or family members. It was the name of an actress." The man laughed heartily. "And coincidentally she happens to be an actress I myself have worshiped for thirty years. I've seen almost all her films. I also own many of her videos. Would you like to see some?"

In this film your name is Catherine Berger. This first name happens to be the same as yours. It must feel strange when your name is identical to that of the character you play. If I were to reveal my real name now, it would appear to me like the name of a fictional character.

Catherine is sitting in a taxi, her face reflected in the rearview mirror above the driver's seat. Like strings of nerves laid bare, she rides between flashy advertisements, hectic pedestrians, and threatening facades. Probably she can no longer bear this city after having spent several years in a cell.

A glimpse back into a past time is depicted in soft blurry colors. Catherine Berger and another woman share a cell that looks like a train compartment for two. She eats lunch in a gigantic dining room where over one hundred women are eating. It would look exactly like a girls' boarding school if the women were younger. Most of them have reached the age of maturity, and a few look really quite old. Catherine Berger and her cellmate appear to have developed the sort of friendship otherwise reserved only for men in the military. There are no men in this institution. Or rather only one: Catherine Berger sometimes receives visits from a polite, well-dressed man. I assume it is his task to defend her juristically. One day she asks him for something and he throws a fit. He refuses, arguing with a swift tongue, and then flees. "She wanted him to give her a child so that when she was released she'd have someone to give her life meaning," the man in the lab coat remarked.

Catherine nods to her friend and with the grace of an athlete slices open her wrists. Her friend shouts for help, as the two of them have planned, and in the next scene the would-be suicide is lying in an infirmary bed. She asks a young janitor who is sweeping the floor beside her bed to accompany her to the bathroom. The young man agrees, and, bored, lights himself a cigarette outside the bathroom door. At the very least he wants to enjoy some nicotine while he is having to wait for the murderer, but she doesn't allow him this respite. She drags him into the toilet stall.

The man in the lab coat started to tell me something about the stall. I didn't understand what he meant. Catherine definitely wanted to have a child in any case; that's why she seduced the young janitor. The young boy Catherine visits as soon as she is released is the child that was conceived in the bathroom.

The man in the lab coat said he had to make a quick phone call. He left me alone in the room with the TV screen.

Catherine is lying in her bedroom. She is being observed through the keyhole by an amorous eye: a situation presumably not so surprising for a woman like her. This eye, however, does not belong to a stranger; it is the eye of her own son. He wants to make his mother into an image he can worship. While the sons of other mothers remain at a distance of only fifty centimeters from them for many years, and therefore forget how to see the entire body of their mother as if she were a painted image, this boy was able to see his mother only in the picture-frame of the keyhole and continues to desire her as on the first day of their reunion, when he kissed the sleeping Catherine on her lips without knowing who she was.

I picked up the remote control and pressed the pause button. Something happened that I had never experienced before: Catherine came to a standstill, her life-story paused, and for the first time I could see every detail of her face. In a movie theater I was never able to stop the images, and so you were always racing into my retina. Now I had the power to stop your movements. I was shocked and ran out of the room without knowing what I meant to do. The door to the room was not locked. There was no one in the corridor who could have helped me. The front door of the building was open, the reception desk unstaffed. Outside on the street there was a bus stop; a bus was just arriving, and it stopped for me. The bus drove off again after I'd boarded.

•

A person who has been arrested is endlessly forced to play the role of prisoner and go on escaping. Every release and every escape are provisional. In all likelihood I was pregnant. If this child were ever to be born, I would have to place it as a sacrificial offering before the screen of a movie theater.

In Indochina you lost your plantation, the house where you were born, your lover, and your adopted daughter. Only the step-grandchild born to your lover and your adopted daughter remained. Perhaps this child was the price your adopted daughter intended to pay for the revolution. I intended to abandon my child in front of the screen and leave the cinema behind, which meant leaving Paris.

I sat down on a park bench, leaned forward until my hair touched the earth, and said to my vagina: "I'm going to leave you. You're staying here. The screen will be your diaper and your milk. I'm leaving, and I'm leaving you here."

Tuong Linh's window was dark. I rang the bell, but there was no response. I imagined him strolling in the sultry night air in Bangkok, thinking of me, unable to figure out a solution since the fragrance of spices and orchids was tickling his nostrils. Then again it couldn't be night there if it was night here. This fact made Tuong Linh seem infinitely far away.

•

Yoko Tawada

I went to the basement where I had lived with Marie. The door wasn't locked. It smelled familiar. In the corner where Marie had always slept, there was a woolen blanket with a pattern of roses. There were no cobwebs anywhere. I sat down on a wooden crate and waited for a long time, but no one came. My eyelids grew heavy. When a moth flew over my head, I had the feeling that I must immediately give it an answer that would sound plausible but reveal nothing.

The next day, while the sun kept shining, I remained in the basement. In the evening I went back to Tuong Linh's building. The window continued to display a dead rectangle of lightlessness. My stomach was aching with hunger, but I had no money. I spied a half-opened Styrofoam container and a newspaper in a garbage can. Pretending I was interested in the headlines, I picked up the plastic container together with the newspaper. In a park I carefully opened the packaging and found one third of a hamburger. I could see traces of lipstick on the white bread. This was a premiere for me; I hesitated for a moment, then resolutely bit into the hamburger and found even the slightly acidic taste of this stranger's lipstick unnaturally tasty. I knew this taste from somewhere. Perhaps I had eaten the lipstick of a strange woman before. Or was it the taste of ketchup and mayonnaise that was greeting my tongue with familiar disgustingness? A dog was running around in the park, ignoring me and my meal. I wanted to return to the basement, and as I got up and started to walk, a wave of dizziness washed over me. The entrails in my abdomen began to burn. I squatted down beside a streetlamp. The blood was leaving my head. A tall African man stood in front of me, watching. This was my last image before the blackout.

The white rectangle was not a screen but the ceiling I lay beneath on a bed. The sheets smelled of strong disinfectant. In the room were several beds; I was surely in a hospital for the poor, maybe even a dungeon. I have to run away, I thought, but I couldn't even get up. A deep nausea emanating not, as was usually the case, from my stomach, but from deep within my abdomen. A dull heartbeat in the distance. My body felt like the body of another person. It had nothing to do with me—the only thing connecting us was pain. "What's the matter?" There was an old man lying beside me. "I have to go home." "Why?" The man, bedded in wrinkles, was calmness personified. From his mouth, even the word "why" sounded reassuring. The two other beds in the room were unoccupied. "Why am I here?" "Don't be sad." Then the old man said a long sentence I didn't understand. Since I didn't react, he repeated the news in a simpler way: "Your child is dead." The old man showed me a slip of paper. "A young man from Senegal saw you lose consciousness on the street. He carried you here on his shoulders. An enormous fellow. This note is from him." I lifted myself up to take the paper from him. My legs were still limp as noodles. On the paper was written "Diop" and a telephone number. I folded up the note carefully, wanting to tuck it away somewhere, but I had neither a purse nor pockets.

When I woke up again, it was pitch black in the room. I no longer felt nauseated. The old man was asleep, one further bed was occupied, and the fourth was still smooth. You couldn't see whether the new, tall person with short hair was a man or a woman. In any case this person was sleeping soundly, and the old man slept as well. A chance to escape. I was wearing white pajamas. Where had they hidden my clothes? Next to the old man's bed stood a chair, and on its back hung a brown cardigan that probably belonged to him. I put it on and buttoned it. Maybe it would look as if I was wearing a wool dress. Shoes were still missing. My naked soles felt the cold linoleum floor. In the hallway, the green signs for the emergency exits were glowing. There was no one at the reception desk. Perhaps the person on duty had left for a moment. There was a small portable television showing a soccer game. I felt ashamed of my naked feet. The buildings around me looked elegantly clothed, whereas I had naked legs and feet. I had to get away from here. The cold asphalt street whipped the soles of my feet with every step. "I have no shoes, no shoes, no shoes," I repeated as I walked, as though this were the only worry I had in life. "Barefoot and uncombed, no roof over my head, no visa in my passport, no passport in my purse, no purse in my hand, no name in my head," I sang quietly to myself. I felt better. The soles of my feet grew warm from walking, and in the sky a few faint lights appeared that might have been stars. Countless rooftops separated people from one another, the illegal from the legal, the sick from the professionally active, the voiceless from the lawmakers, but the great roof of the Parisian sky was something we all had in common. I found this almost impossible to believe, that even you were probably sleeping somewhere beneath this sky. It no longer seemed unbearable to me to be wandering around in the nocturnal city. Why should I always squeeze myself in between a roof and a pair of shoes when freedom was not yet outlawed? My head suddenly felt as free as my feet. I surely looked exhausted, sick, and dirty, but I walked on in good spirits, waiting for the next film that might be shown on the enormous screen of the nocturnal sky.

At the edge of the road I spotted three plump garbage bags. I opened each of them in turn and discovered papers that smelled of beef, envelopes that had been written on and then torn up, a small, elegant hat for a doll, cigarette butts, aluminum foil from prepackaged coffee, a ballpoint pen, a banana peel, and hair of different colors. Patiently I looked for something for my feet and finally dug out a pair of plastic sandals. The soles were worn down, but they were still serviceable. Suddenly I was weary and didn't want to walk another step. I crept into the courtyard of a building and made myself small and round between the bicycles to sleep.

The next morning I had no desire to remember who I was. My legs automatically moved in the direction from which the sounds of cars were streaming. The street sign said "rue des Pyrénées." My legs immediately knew that they should simply walk down this street to the south and then turn right at the large intersection to return to Marie's basement. Instead I shunned this and the other larger thoroughfares to avoid the gaze of strangers. I trudged through little alleyways, trying not to lose my sense of direction, which wasn't easy as these narrow alleys never ran parallel to the major streets.

Once again my eyes fell upon a partly eaten hamburger. My belly growled. I no longer felt any nausea, even though the food tasted of ketchup and mayonnaise. And I no longer felt any pain in my abdomen. Still, the song of mourning that refused to become a melody covered my skin like damp netting.

In the evening I arrived at the familiar entrance to the basement. When the door creaked, a hoarse female voice asked something from inside. Before me appeared a gaunt woman with silver hair. Though I could see I was disturbing her, she didn't seem as dismissive as I feared. "I'm looking for

Marie. Marie and I lived here together six years ago." The woman's face changed as quickly as shrimp crackers in hot oil. "It's me! I'm Marie!" she cried, taking my hands. Her palms were rough but warm and somewhat moist. In her face I discovered many new lines that hadn't been there before. But when I called her name again, only the old lines remained on the surface, and the new ones vanished.

Chapter Nine

Les voleurs

In the basement I dreamed a great deal. In one dream I was a child, and the city I lived in was a harbor town. An orphan has no right to hide. Look, look, look at her! How cute! How thin! How sweet! How sickly! Hair like a bird's nest, legs like brown asparagus! Look, look, look at her! This girl has been abandoned, she is free—free to anyone who wants her!

Only in the darkness of the movie theater was I protected from the eyes of others. My cinema was a "Ma," she wrapped me in her mucous membranes. She shielded me from the sun, from the force of visibility. Life was being played out on the screen, a life before death. People fought there, or else slept together. They cried and sweated, and the screen remained dry. The cinema, its stage, had no depth, but it did have its own light source.

Your name is Marie and this time you aren't a prostitute—you're a professor of philosophy. With a book in your hand you speak to the students in the lecture hall. The microphone inclines toward your mouth like an insectivore. The lecture hall is packed to bursting; the students sit shoulder to shoulder. One is constantly moving his pen, another is trying to shake the pebbles out of his brain, a third is observing the speaker's beauty with dreamy eyes.

I envied these students, and my old dream occurred to me once more: I wanted to study at the university, to study philosophy, something I had wanted to do even back before I learned to blow my own nose properly.

Instead of studying, I wandered around the city all day long: no roof over my head, illegal and unemployed, a mute creature devoid of language skills, unwashed and lethargic. In the rue des Écoles I discovered a book by Plato in a shop window. I didn't know anything about him, but his name had been familiar to me since childhood. A school friend whose parents owned a pension in Saigon once gave me

Yoko Tawada

the paperback edition of *The Symposium*, which one of the French guests had left behind in a room. I put the book on my desk and looked at the title every day. "Le banquet"—I knew exactly what the word meant, and imagined a large ballroom with chandeliers. Translucent noodles, red prawns, bean sprouts, cilantro, and lemongrass were spread across a large, round table. Delicacies in the shape of rolls and little balls filled white porcelain bowls and large silver platters. A ball, a huge ball the size of my head or even bigger keeps growing, a dangerous ball. Suddenly a chef appears and slices the ball in two with his knife.

A few women wore traditional dresses, *áo dài* of supple silk, while others wore elegant French evening gowns. They circled about, moving from one point to another as if dancing a *ronde* whenever they wished to find new conversation partners or wineglasses. That was the banquet, and I wasn't there; I was standing outside in the street, the light of the chandeliers was seeping through the window, casting my shadow on the paving stones.

I couldn't follow your lecture. All I recognized was the word "aggression." Aggression, agronomy, agricultural technology—an uncle of mine had studied agricultural technology in the GDR—culture, agriculture, angry, agreement. I had always thought I couldn't speak a word of English, but I had only imagined this. A soldier once asked me on the street in Saigon: "Do you agree with me?" I was just a child.

Should I agree with my not being invited to the banquet and remain docile, or should I fly into a rage and smash the ballroom window?

I knew the word "aggression" because it was one of the French words Ai Van sometimes used to incorporate into her Vietnamese sentences. I rarely thought of Ai Van, but this word brought her voice back to my ear.

Juliette doesn't look like a student, but she is studying at the university. She is taking one of Marie's classes. Someone must have told her where to get an application form, how to pay the tuition fees, which books to read, and with what casualness or reserve one speaks with the professors.

Juliette, a wildcat in heat, takes a bottle of perfume from a shelf, quickly puts it in her handbag and leaves the shop without paying. Juliette is being dragged off by three policemen; she's biting their hands, juicy police hands, smoked male hands, crunchy meaty hands. Juliette thrashes around on all fours on the floor, the three policemen trying to hold her down. While the sympathetic policeman Alex is interrogating her, she observes him with the intelligence of an untamed beast, calculating her chances of survival down to the last millimeter. She asks him for a cigarette—an impertinent, flirtatious request as she knows perfectly well the man feels drawn to her. He takes care of the formalities and the wildcat is free to go. "Do you really want to let her go?" one of his colleagues asks in surprise. "Yes, let her go," he replies.

Alex, the little brother of a car dealer who works at night, Alex, the son of an important Mafia boss, Alex, the ascetic policeman who hates criminals, not because he's Catholic but because he hates his brother.

Juliette lies in wait for Alex. He ignores her and gets into his car. Juliette quickly slips in through the other door and sits down in the passenger seat. Alex reaches for the gear shift, and she reaches for his trousers and the object within them. His eyes are like the eyes of a hare looking down the black hole of a rifle barrel. An exchange of words between them like an exchange of money, one bad currency in exchange for another. Then the two are already in a bedroom. In a film one can land in bed so quickly. Out the window one sees a bit of suburban landscape with highway signs. Juliette is wearing a summer dress, Alex a white shirt—only from the waist down are they naked. They have sex with powerful thrusts, a painful, frantic coupling full of rage. They do not fully undress, they do not kiss, they do not smile, caress one another, or speak. A cockfight of the sexual organs, pure, unadulterated intercourse with no gourmet digressions, as if they'd both confessed to being nothing more than pure, holy, sexual beings.

Juliette is sitting with Marie in the bathtub, smiling like a helpless girl. In warm water, bodies forget all the constraints of buttons, elastic bands, belts, and zippers. The two bodies lose their contours, dissolve. They are no longer touching, though they are still connected through the element of water. Water: the language of the unconstrained.

Juliette turns her back to Marie. Marie's hands embrace Juliette from behind. Marie takes the showerhead and rinses Juliette's hair. A baptism for a nameless religion without beliefs. Juliette shuts her eyes and luxuriates in the warm flowing-away that leaves nothing behind. She believes in nothing.

It wasn't the first time your name was Marie. You revived the girl in the bathtub. This is the same bathtub in which you once, as Carol, laid the corpse of the man you had murdered.

Juliette is surrounded by many male eyes. The eyes of the policeman Alex are windowpanes made of frozen tears; the eyes of his brother are glasses filled with golden whiskey. This brother knows how to transport money from another pocket to his own, never the other way around. His suit is made of soft fabric, sumptuous permanent press, his neckties are flowery, his men jump to open the door for him. I have everything I take everything I have you and many other women I have money I give you a lot of this money I give you not everything but many of the many things you stay here you cannot leave you know too much you must come deeper inside until you can no longer return.

I heard the word *projet* several times from Marie's lips. The word "love," on the other hand, could almost never be heard, although I knew this word in French. Most likely it had gotten buried in compounds with other words. The project existed all alone. A project is a promise, a sketch for a house that can be lived in, to which one can invite one's friends. How different I would have been if I'd had a project. But a creature of the streets has no project—always only the selfsame activity that is monotonously repeated. Marie suggests a project to Juliette, a joyful, intelligent project that transforms an alley into the Milky Way. Juliette doesn't seem too interested.

Juliette puts on her black leather jacket. It smells of criminality. The criminal is a smell, a whisper in the dark, a hiding, a made-up name, an insomniac nervous system, a knife, an endless list of names in one's head, a running away, a mixed feeling of fear and sentimentality created by the sight of the faint reflection of lights on the train tracks at night. Criminality is my smell.

Juliette puts on her black leather jacket. The leather gleams like the night, the night in which one of the men cuts through a chain with bolt cutters. The gate to the lot provides access to the freight trains loaded with new cars. With practiced hands, the men remove the wedges from beneath the car tires. Then two guards appear and shine a flashlight in Juliette's face. Juliette raises both hands and freezes. The guards hold their pistols pointed at her and slowly approach. Suddenly a shot is heard, and a shootout begins. Juliette jumps out of the car and throws herself down. One of the guards falls, the other manages to escape. The boss is on the ground, covered in blood. Juliette looks at him; he cannot get up on his own.

A bell rings, Marie opens the door, and there is Juliette, her face half cut off by the door, Marie's lips move toward Juliette's lips, Juliette refuses, utters angry words and drinks bitter red wine while Marie continues to fuss over her and speak about a meaningful project, projects are always meaningful, Marie tries to encourage Juliette, console her, love her, but Juliette turns away, Marie falls silent, Juliette smashes her wine glass against the edge of the sink, her lips eat the shards of glass, bloody lips, a sliced-up tongue, she drinks the splinters, she drinks death, Marie rushes to her side, uses force to open her bloody mouth, removes the shards of glass, the wildcat bites Marie's fingers, she screams

Yoko Tawada

but her fingers don't stop, Marie's white sweater is red with blood, shards fall to the floor, tears, an embrace, cut.

You carry around a small, flat container everywhere you go. You don't swallow shards of glass, but you do swallow a golden liquid and white pills. You swallow and drink and throw up. If things go on like this, you will one day arrive at the square called "Place Vendôme." But of course this isn't you it's a role you're playing, I know this. Who is it if it isn't you? If a woman lives in me, she cannot be simply a Marie or a Marianne. Who is she?

Alex invites Marie to dinner and cooks for her, places flowers on the table. Juliette has vanished since the incident at the freight depot. Alex pours his guest a glass of red wine, they talk and laugh. The bottle is empty. Marie faints. Alex tends to her after snapping a picture of the sleeping beauty. This holy image remains in his room, just as I keep a photo of you beside my bed. All of us worship Marie the Holy One.

    Alex was already in love with you once before, in another movie, though at that time he was still your brother. Actors have to lose their memories after every film. They forget what they used to be and think the audience has forgotten too.

There is a story about a girl who lost her parents and brother during the Vietnam War. The parents died. The girl was raised by one family and never learned that her brother was still alive and growing up in another family. The girl became a woman, met a man and married him. They had two children. One day as the couple was taking a bath together, the man began speaking of his earliest childhood memory. The woman turned pale, ran out of the bathroom, left the house and never returned.

This episode has nothing to do with the film. It just occurred to me at this moment.

When I imagined having a love affair with my brother, I immediately felt sick to my stomach as if I'd contracted fever from poisonous insect stings.

Marie is gone, possibly dead. She left behind a yellow parcel. "La poste" is stamped on a cardboard box one can buy at any post office. The post office continues to exist after the movie is over, and even after we are dead—undeliverable packages will still be stored there. Marie's package contains a notebook belonging to her and cassettes with Juliette's voice on them.

Juliette flees to a harbor town and finds a job at a bookstore. Alex drives there and goes into the shop but hides behind a bookshelf. Juliette has changed. Now she is a woman who wakes up each morning at the same time and drinks coffee from the same cup. She no longer sleeps with policemen,

176   *Yoko Tawada*

no longer takes baths with her professor, no longer steals perfume. Alex leaves the shop without speaking to her.

If I had visited Juliette, I would have taken all the Plato books off the shelves and thrown them at her. Why didn't you come to the banquet? Why did you abandon Marie? What has become of the wildcat scent? Where is the thinking water? What's the point of this final scene? Where should we send the cassettes?

Two women have become one, and once more you were the one who vanished.

Fortunately the other Marie hadn't gone missing. Thanks to Marie, the raw skin of my emotions became somewhat smoother every day. The pedestrians I saw on the street were broken gramophones, the city itself an unsuccessful film, but I went on sleeping in the basement and living in the movie theaters.

Marie told me she was receiving unemployment benefits. She also worked as a custodian in public spaces and was even able to save some of her earnings. "I always took my work seriously," she said, laughing at the word "work." I, on the other hand, was a baby chick that sat at home waiting for food. Marie fed me and gave me pocket money and said I should go to the movies. I thought: things can't go on like this, but I didn't know how to earn money. It no longer frightened me to be alone in the basement since my skin was taking on a color similar to its walls. Even the pressure and heat swirling inside my head no longer bothered me.

I convinced myself that I would have to concentrate my energies before I could take the next step. I had put prison and the hospital behind me. Now I had the right to enjoy the exalted state of convalescence. A dignified gleam illuminated this basement hole thanks to the name Marie.

On nights when Marie didn't return to the basement, I consorted in my head with policeman Alex. Following Juliette's example, I greedily summoned all my memories of this utilizable pain, every scrap. I felt a mild ache, particularly when I thought of how the policeman could be such a dog. Like Juliette, I was in search of unadulterated contact between organs, a contact free of longing, for you were the one and only object of my passion. Of course I was unworthy of making your acquaintance. The very thought of standing before you filled me with shame. Perhaps Juliette had felt much the same thing. Of all the men around her, she didn't love a single one—she loved only something that was embodied by Marie. Juliette, though, felt like a piece of garbage in her presence. In school I had learned that one should not let oneself be governed by false modesty, but in this case nothing else was possible. And anyway, even though it was unbearable to feel smaller and smaller when

Yoko Tawada

compared to you, it was also a pleasure. It was at most as a dog that I would be able to remain by your side. The sum total of happiness Juliette would derive from her new profession as a bookseller and the family she would eventually start could not surpass the happiness of this dog.

But not every dog can be so lucky. Would I even be chosen by you if I were a dog? What sort of dog should I become? How could I become a dog? There was a film where you play the role of a dog for a while. Or more precisely: you play the role of a woman who's playing a dog. Unfortunately I never saw this film. Therefore I couldn't learn from it. When it was drizzling, I would think a great deal about living as a dog. When the skies were clear, my opinion would quickly change, and then it would seem that perhaps it would be better to study at the university.

Chapter Ten

Le dernier métro

The uniformed and jackbooted soldiers are speaking German. At the hotel reception desk, on the street, even in the theater, everywhere one finds them standing around saying, "I don't speak French." The voices arrive from far away. Behind the sound of this language, another life of mine was buried. Sometimes I was seized by an urgent desire to return to the GDR, to undo everything that had happened. If only I had acted differently then ... If I hadn't gone to that Russian band's concert ... If

I hadn't exchanged frivolous words with a stranger from Bochum ... If I hadn't drunk that vodka ... But I could no longer return, for the GDR had long since ceased to exist.

When I came out of the métro station Odéon, I was encircled by a handful of men and women who looked like students. I wanted to run away, but I heard the sentence: "We're from the university." I nodded, since after all I wanted to go there myself. "We're from a student theater and are looking for an Asian actress." Two men, three women. One of the women began to explain an array of things to me with great enthusiasm: the university, communication, culture, solidarity, the theater, literature, politics. Her words joined hands to form a whirlwind that spiralled around me. This could be my first step toward entering the university, I thought, and so nodded quickly twice in succession. We went together to a café, where the woman placed a booklet in my hand. It was a somewhat crookedly stapled copy of the play. In the dramatis personae I found the Vietnamese name "Phuong Lien"; the rest of the names were French-sounding, like Arlette, Nadine, Rosette, and Bernard. One of the men introduced himself to me as the director. I couldn't understand his name and lacked the courage to ask him to repeat it. "Actually, Lucas was our director, but he can't come anymore. So now I'm directing." The name of the director who would no longer be coming was easy for me to retain. Why couldn't Lucas come any longer?

Yoko Tawada

Immediately I began to think about this absent person although I didn't even know him.

Every evening at seven I went to rehearsals that took place in a small, moldy space. The others attended seminars at the university during the day. I would have liked to ask them questions about their studies, but never found the right moment to do so. During every rehearsal there would be one fifteen-minute break when everyone hastily lit their Gauloises and drank pitch-black coffee, speaking twice as fast as they did on stage. The contents of their conversations, along with their individual facial expressions, were obscured by the thick cigarette smoke. I loved the smell of the Gauloises, but was afraid of the name as it reminded me of an old tiger. I preferred not smoking to uttering the name at a kiosk.

My lines consisted of short sentences in which the words were placed next to each other without anything holding them together. People probably thought this was how immigrants talked. I expended little effort learning my lines by heart, but it took a lot of courage for me to speak the lines aloud. The first sentence of the day I would utter with my eyes closed as if leaping off a cliff. The moment I finished the sentence, everyone would jump in to correct my pronunciation. My words had never before attracted so much attention as they did here at these rehearsals.

I screamed, "Leave me alone!" without meaning it at all. That's only what my lines said. My lips burned hotly all the same. Speaking meant wrenching one's mouth wide open or pursing the lips to form a narrow passage for air and forcing the breath out violently or rubbing the consonants against the mucous membranes of the throat or discovering new sinus cavities behind the nose. Especially difficult for me was the art known as aspiration. When I forgot it at the necessary point, I would be criticized at once. I didn't understand the rule, I thought it should be possible for people to peer into my head and see the caesuras I was inwardly placing.

At first I kept my new job as an actress secret from Marie. I ended up telling her two weeks later as she was looking worried watching me prepare to go out. "It's a student group, but they have a rehearsal space. And all of them have a good heart for good things," I added, as though I needed a justification. "That's wonderful. What sort of story is the play?" Marie asked. I couldn't tell her the plot of the play because I didn't understand it yet. So I simply began to recite my lines. Marie burst out laughing, and I felt hurt—it had never occurred to me that my lines might be comical.

I appeared in three scenes. In the first, I was surrounded by women who were asking me questions, and I struggled to answer them. Then I remained alone on stage and spoke a broken monologue. In the second scene, a burly man in a suit approached me, grabbed me by the collar, and asked me questions. This man, whose name began with a "D," was being played by the director as this character only appeared once. In the last scene, I had to lie on the floor the whole time. The others tried to wake me, but I remained motionless, probably dead. After this, the play ended happily without me.

I had never visited a theater house in Paris, though the setting was familiar to me from the films in which you played the role of a stage actress. I particularly liked you when you were working at a theater. The screen in the cinema was a naked illusion that immediately drew me into its space, while I could measure, accept, and enjoy my distance from you when you were standing on a stage. Once I took a walk in Montparnasse to find the theater where you worked in the role of Marion Steiner.

Strangely, I began to develop a hatred for the burly man in the suit, Monsieur D., who grabbed me by the collar every day and bared his teeth. I knew it was only a play, yet it was all I could do to keep my arms from violently shoving him away. "You must look intimidated and paralyzed and keep mute," said this man, suddenly switching into the role of director. I felt annoyed at his tone of voice and simply looked away. "You acted better in the beginning. Why can't you do any better now?"

After the rehearsal, Nadine and Rosette sometimes asked me whether I wasn't cold in my thin clothing or what plans I had for the evening. Only Arlette acted as if I didn't exist. She quickly changed her clothes, lit her cigarette, and went to join the men. The director usually brought her home on his motorcycle. I thought she was in love with him until one day I surprised Arlette and Nadine in the women's bathroom. They were standing there half undressed, caressing one another's breasts, drawing circles upon them with their palms. Later I was no longer sure if I wasn't remembering this scene from one of your movies.

Once, we had a visitor. He stood with his arms crossed and his lips closed, observing the rehearsal from beginning to end. He occasionally scratched his right thigh as if he'd been stung there by an insect. The visitor was a university professor and had recently returned from the U.S., the director told us later. After the rehearsal, the professor came up to me and said I'd done a wonderful job. I realized that it had been a long time since anyone had praised me.

Once I happened to run into Nadine at the movies. The film's story was set in a theater house. Lukas, the theater's artistic director, is hiding in the basement because he is of

Jewish descent and this is World War II. You are playing the director's wife, Marion Steiner.

Marion continues her work as a stage actress. In the evening she sits in the office, wrestling with mountains of paperwork to keep the theater above water. With a pale, overworked face she opens the door to a little room. There stand two of the women who work for her, in the act of tasting each other's lips. One of them becomes hysterical, begs Marion to forgive her, weeps. Presumably this woman worships Marion but consorts with another woman who is easier to handle. And even the new male actor who's just been hired appears to worship Marion, but nonetheless chases after other women. Only on stage does he dare to declare his love to Marion: day after day with exactly the same words.

In this film your face appears narrow and pale. It no longer has the vitality and body temperature of your face in *Indochine*. *Indochine* was also made twelve years before. The more recent the film, the younger you look. As Marion, you appear to be a fragile bridge between the girl Carol in London and the mature woman Eliane in Indochina.

Nadine was sitting right behind me. I didn't notice her until the film was over when she spoke to me. She invited me for an ice cream and asked me if I selected the movies I went to see according to their subject matter or by director. I immediately replied: "The actress is important." Nadine laughed, gave an embarrassed cough, and told me about a lecture that might interest me. She was currently attending a seminar on media art that was hosting a public lecture the next week. I should come, she said.

The lecture was being given by a young academic whose head motions reminded me of a canary. It was difficult for me to follow what she was saying. During the lecture, she showed slides with scenes from several films. My eyes were riveted when I saw you in one of them. You were dressed in white and inserted into an exotic landscape. *Mississippi Mermaid*, *Africans*, and *Touche pas à la femme blanche* were the titles of these films, I later learned. "Exotisme" and "orientalisme" were the only words in the lecture I definitely understood. As for the rest, I couldn't say what I did or didn't understand, but when the concluding words were spoken and the discussion began, I suddenly raised my hand and asked: "And *Indochine*? What about *Indochine*?" I myself couldn't comprehend how I had suddenly become so impertinent as to ask a question at a university. The face of the lecturer beamed as if I'd put my finger right on the crux of the matter. She talked and talked until the audience became restless. I understood not a single word of her response, but this no longer mattered.

•

It was raining. I went to rehearsal carrying my saggy umbrella that I'd bought very cheaply near the Gare du Nord. The director walked up to me and abruptly asked if I possessed a valid residency permit. He was transformed into Monsieur D., the unpleasant character in the play who insolently interrogated me. Arlette walked over to us and observed the situation like a street fight. "Do you have a residency permit?" "No." "Do you have a passport?" "No." Arlette raised her eyebrows. The face of the director vanished from my consciousness—I heard only his voice. "There were policemen here before. They were asking about you. They said they were coming back. It would be better if you went home right away." At this moment Nadine ran into the rehearsal room: "They're coming!" The director opened the back door of the room, pressed a key into my hand and pointed to the stairs. "Go into the very last room, where the props are stored. Then lock the door from inside and wait quietly until we come to get you. Don't turn on the light." I went down the stairs, crept along the narrow hallway, and opened the last door. Soon my eyes grew accustomed to the darkness and recognized shapes consisting of crosses, angles, corners, bars, and hooks. I was standing among props not currently in use.

After a long time the director tapped on the door. "Now you can come out. Where's the key? Give it back to me." In the rehearsal room, the others were waiting for us. They didn't run to greet me, they didn't hug me, they didn't console me. All of them were paralyzed with their own worries. "We've been informed about your past. Starting tomorrow you can't come anymore. Otherwise they'll arrest you." "What about my role?" "We'll have to find someone else." The director's cheeks were purple; Bernard and Rosette hung their heads; Arlette walked nervously back and forth as if she wanted to start doing something else right away. And Nadine was staring out the window with an insulted expression, as if I had betrayed her.

I stopped in front of a shop window containing a large number of bottles. There was something trapped in them, perhaps people who had been transformed into liquid. The contents of the bottles were mostly white or gold, though in one bottle the liquid was a dull caramel color, in another green. An old man with a blue apron stuck his head out of the shop and asked me something. "*Pardon?*" He repeated the question. The third time around I understood he was asking me the name of my father. But why would a liquor store owner want to know my father's name? I was getting nervous. He persisted. I shouted: "Ho Chi Minh!" Satisfied, the man gave a nod, pointed to the sky with one finger, and placed a heavy bottle in my hand. On the label I read: "Gorbatschow." He laughed, and I laughed as well, but for no reason. Then I tried to give him back the bottle, which was shaped like a Russian church, but he said it was mine. "Why?" I held out the bottle to him. He pushed it back toward me, repeating that it was mine.

On the label beneath the name "Gorbatschow" was the word "Berlin." The sound of this name made my body start to quake with fever and chills. I soon discovered that Monsieur Gorbatschow was a healer. After the first swallow, my blood awakened, my lungs immediately filled with pride, my temples flushed with fresh inspiration. Unfortunately there was no dance floor in the basement where these new ideas could manifest themselves. So I began tapping against the wall with two fingers that were meant to represent the legs of a dancer. They had neither a torso nor a mouth, just two legs dancing in the air. The Gorbatschow basement theater had no audience. Nonetheless, I held it in higher esteem than that ridiculous student theater. I was a born actress. I didn't wish to follow the example of Tristana, who was poisoned by her own brown bitterness, or of Carol lying unconscious among overturned furniture. I didn't want to drown like Professor Marie in a Mediterranean made of whiskey. I wanted to be like spirits rising up from the bottle to rescue a woman like Marie from her thoughts of suicide. I wanted to survive the war like Marion. The place of this survival was called the theater. What sort of play should be performed? I didn't know the play Marion was staging between the cherry orchard and the magic mountain to sustain her during wartime. When the war was over, Marion stood on stage to receive the applause of the cheering audience. To her right was her husband, to her left her lover. She held them in her two hands like suitcases.

Gorbatschow caused a side effect that might detract from his fame. When I woke up, my bones had lost their density and my hair was hanging down lusterless. I felt an urgent need to ingest something, and frantically searched for the unknown food I was lacking. Meat perhaps? Marie had brought me "sweet and sour pork" from her favorite fast food restaurant, but that didn't satisfy me. Chocolate perhaps? Even this black, magical item brought me no strength. In the end I just went on drinking Gorbatschow. At once I felt extremely motivated to do something, for example to read books, learn new vocabulary words, become prettier, and venture out into the city to attend a theater performance. But my engine wouldn't start. I couldn't even manage to get up and look out the barred window. I simply remained flat on the mattress Marie had found in a heap of trash on the street.

The bottle was soon empty. If I were to return to the shop and utter the magic words "Ho Chi Minh," perhaps the man would give me another Gorbatschow. No, I'd better just go to the movies and visit my temple, my Pantheon, my pagoda. My feet, however, automatically chose the street which contained no movie theater but only the shop in question. Today, the man who had given me the Gorbatschow wasn't behind the counter; instead it was a saleswoman with a long, narrow throat. She wouldn't give me anything. I would have to pay. What did a Gorbatschow cost? I didn't really want the bottle, but felt it was urgently necessary to find out the exact price.

While I was observing the saleswoman from the sidewalk, a boy appeared out of nowhere, grabbed two bottles of wine and ran away. The saleswoman jumped out of the shop and sprinted after him with unexpected speed. I went into the shop and found the bottle I was looking for on the shelf behind the cash register. No price tag was visible. I took down the bottle and rotated it 180 degrees. If I had found the price, I would have waited for the saleswoman's return and paid the amount in question. But since I couldn't find one, I took the bottle with me and went home.

I was happy while I was drinking, and I understood that the word happiness contained a chemical significance. A few days later I discovered the miniature edition of Gorbatschow, which I could afford to buy with my pocket money. I placed each empty bottle in the garbage can on the street so Marie would be none the wiser.

Whenever I walked down the steps leading to the métro, the passersby lost their colors. Even the columns and posters withdrew into the mood of a black-and-white film. I walked back up the steps, trying to imagine the steps covered with a bright red carpet. I wished to keep ascending, to rise up higher and higher.

Chapter Eleven

Place Vendôme

I ascended the gray steps. My body was being marinated in some kind of painful fluid and had grown heavy. My head was spinning. At some point I had begun to make a habit of letting my belly hang down as I climbed stairs, like a pregnant woman. But my child had been buried long ago, without my ever having seen it. What I carried in my womb was no longer a child, it was something different.

The last métro must have long since reached its sleeping place. The last passenger had already departed—the only thing drifting about in the banquet hall was cold cigarette smoke. Was Plato at the party again? What did he talk about this time? Did he speak French, in other words, was the conversation dubbed or were there subtitles? The philosopher went home with Professor Marie Leblanc. Along the way, the two of them had a passionate discussion on the relationship between aggression and boiled eggs. Your erotic appeal consisted of your intelligence. By Indochina at the latest this was clear to me. The banquet had long since ended. Between the plates smeared with sauce, knives, forks, and spoons lay scattered. Here and there stood empty or half-empty wineglasses. I began to collect the leftover red wine from several glasses into one glass. When this glass was full, I drank it down. Even without a mirror I knew what this looked like. The film *Place Vendôme* had already shown me. At the time, your weary body was surrounded by money and diamonds that belonged to other people. You wandered about in the splendid hall of a financial institution. In this film you owned neither a rubber plantation nor a theater. You only possessed a few diamonds whose origins were sketchy. These stones reflected an immeasurable radiance, but since they did not have birth certificates, nobody wanted them.

In the morning I felt like vomiting, and crept secretly out of the basement so Marie wouldn't notice. On the street I saw a group of children and a woman with a fresh-baked baguette under her arm. I threw up at the side of the road. A student walking by made a face. She was holding a bottle of Evian. The transparent plastic container glittered in the morning sun. Suddenly I wanted to drink pure water. Not the usual tap water from the bathroom of a movie theater I generally drank to quench my thirst. I followed the student in the hope that she might throw away her bottle without having finished it. I imagined rescuing the bottle from the garbage and loudly gulping down the radiance of the water. The student was carrying a briefcase in her other hand, and a brown handbag hung from her shoulders. She walked past several métro stations and bus stops and, not pausing at the gate with the placard reading "Sorbonne," walked tirelessly on. My legs were already quite weary. In front of a café, three Vietnamese-looking young men sat at a table talking. When the word "Doimoi" struck my ear, I forgot the Evian bottle and remained standing at the café. After hesitating for a moment, I sat down at the next table. The men glanced at me questioningly as I studied the menu. I decided to give up my movie that day and ordered an espresso. It seemed ridiculously disproportionate that the same sum that allows one to sit for two entire hours bathed in the image of your face could purchase only a miniscule cup of coffee. The prices of goods had nothing to do with logic. Ho Chi Minh hadn't taught me that—my own experience did.

One of the three Vietnamese men lived in Paris, the other two were tourists. They casually ordered six open-faced sandwiches and a bottle of Beaujolais. The travelers were excitedly talking about a "Condom Café" that had opened in Saigon the year before. I had no idea what that could be. "And Monsieur Kentucky with his chickens has arrived in Saigon as well." They laughed softly, lighting one cigarette after the other. I became nervous, even a little irritable, to hear them speaking of a Saigon that was unknown to me.

After a while the one Vietnamese man who lived in Paris got up and said he had to go, that he needed to stop by the Goethe Institute. "Where? What are you doing there?" "They're planning a concert with a Vietnamese musician who lives in Cologne, and they want to use a photo I took for the posters and programs. I've shot a lot of portraits of this musician." "We'll come with you—we're just bored tourists. Just please don't expect us to speak German on top of everything else. French is already too much for us." The two of them laughed in a carefree way, and with elegant motions of their fingers placed banknotes on the little plate the waiter had brought the bill on.

"Were you ever in Berlin?" one of the tourists asked the photographer. "Yes, of course, three times now. After 1989 the city changed completely." "As much as Saigon?" "It's hard to say. In Berlin you no longer know where you are, and Saigon you simply can't recognize." I quickly paid for my espresso and ran after the three men.

They went into a building that aroused my curiosity. I waited outside in front of an advertising pillar. When they came out half an hour later and vanished around the next corner, I entered the building. In its entrance hung posters announcing films that would be shown. In vain I sought your name.

"Are you looking for the library?" a woman behind me asked in German. I panicked, lost my footing, and was caught by two sturdy arms. "Are you looking for the library?" the voice asked in French. I had an odd feeling that I'd understood the question the first time. I nodded, although I didn't know what I would do at the library. The woman took my hand and drew me after her like a child: a ticklish sensation I hadn't felt for years. "What book are you looking for?" Colorful books of various sizes lined the room. The titles on their spines were made of letters with square shoulders that lacked hooks, roofs and tails. "What subject are you interested in?" "Indochina," I replied spontaneously, since no other word occurred to me at that moment. The woman seemed delighted with my answer; she pulled my hand further back through the shelves until we were standing in the section of less colorful books. "Indochina, Indochina, Indochina ..." the woman repeated under her breath while her fingers scurried over the spines. After a while she groaned with disappointment. It seemed embarrassing to her that she couldn't give me a book. "Come back next week," she said. "I'll have a book for you."

It was absurd to return to the Institute since the entire episode concerning my search for a book about Indochina was
a lie. Plus I couldn't read German. Upon further reflection,
however, peering at illegible books was better than sitting
alone in the basement with Gorbatschow. During the day
I didn't feel prepared to go to the movies. In the evening I
could escape to your latest film, but Marianne, the woman
you play in this movie, was no help to me. She remains limp
on the sofa amid empty wine bottles. A plump, gentle man
touches her thighs. She doesn't respond, sinking silently
into a slumber that will not refresh her.

I was astonished that even in this helpless creature I could
recognize your traits as I knew them from your other films.
It was as if all the directors had come to an agreement
beforehand so that an umbrella character could emerge
to link together the different roles. As if you had already
written a screenplay for your life when you were a child
and later only accepted roles that fit into it. As if you had
always been controlling the making of these films from
behind the scenes with invisible threads.

A thin young woman with a narrow face and long hair is
changing clothes in her office. As she is standing in her
underwear, Marianne appears, catching her by surprise. The
young woman observes the intruder skeptically. Perhaps she

senses that Marianne once had a love affair with the man who is now her lover. Marianne speaks into her unprotected naked skin—not a reproach, not words of scorn, not a threat. On the contrary, Marianne confides a secret to the young woman so she won't fall into a trap. The woman doesn't listen.

The woman who brought me to the library was named Frau Finder. The glasses on her face I had never seen before. The two outer pointed edges of the frames, inlaid with tiny gemstones, curved diagonally upward. These flamboyant glasses seemed at odds with the unpainted, warm-hearted impression the woman otherwise made. In the eyes of Frau Finder, who wore these glasses, I at last became a person who was permitted to touch books without having to run away. When Frau Finder asked me a question, I renounced my freedom to tell a lie. It had been a long time since I'd attempted to answer questions without lying. Speaking without lying felt like sitting on a chair that was missing a leg. I was even having to lie to Marie as she couldn't accept my relationship with Gorbatschow. Frau Finder wasn't horrified at all by my ignorance of German and my poor French. She kept looking for books about Indochina. She even asked her niece, who was studying in Cologne, to look in the university library. "Were you born in Vietnam?" she asked me, and I couldn't lie. "Yes. I also lived in Germany. Only for a year, in Bochum." "Is that so?" Out of joy, Frau

Finder's mouth became an oval. "I'm from Essen, that isn't far from Bochum." She showed me where Essen was on the map on the wall. The left edge of the map ended with "Aachen." Paris wasn't on the map. At the right edge I saw the final stop, "Zittau." Moscow was surely much farther to the east.

I visited Frau Finder once a week. I also attended three film screenings at the Institute. But these films were inaccessible to me because there was no one in them I could speak to.

One day Frau Finder rushed to meet me with a serious expression on her face and asked me if I could return the next afternoon at three—someone wanted to see me. It occurred to me that I had once told Frau Finder of my dream of working at a theater. No doubt she'd found a theater group for me. The next day I showed up at the Institute early, at 2:30 p.m. In front of the building a man stood smoking. A face from a frozen picture rose up and thawed, overlapping with his face in recognition. "Now I've got you," said the voice of this man in the language that was inseparable from it. I watched his cigarette burn out on its own. Frau Finder came out and rapidly explained everything to me: One day this man had seen a classified ad in the Bochum newspaper saying that a Vietnamese doctor in Paris had lost a Vietnamese woman who under complex circumstances had traveled via East Berlin to Bochum in

1988. Anyone who knew her was requested to get in touch with him. Jörg immediately sent a letter written in English to Paris and then received a photograph of me from Tuong Linh. Jörg traveled to Paris, visited the young doctor, and exchanged information with him, though neither of them could get anywhere with their investigations. Jörg didn't give up; he kept visiting Paris during every vacation. He hoped to be able to locate me with the help of his own two legs and visited Vietnamese restaurants, boutiques, language schools, and the embassy. At some point he gave up inwardly, but his legs could no longer stop wandering through Paris. A few days ago he happened to pass by the Institute, wandered in out of curiosity, and started speaking with Frau Finder. She told him she knew a Vietnamese woman who used to live in Bochum.

Jörg was still carrying around the very same briefcase made out of leather that looked like the skin of my parents. He pulled a train ticket out of his case and said: "I'll buy a ticket like this for you, too." Frau Finder translated everything Jörg said slowly, one sentence at a time. Often I didn't understand her French, though it still felt reassuring to me to be told everything twice. The ticket read "Paris/Bochum." The printed letters made the name "Paris" appear like some far-distant city. Then the distinctive smell of an airport suddenly overwhelmed me; someone set off an alarm. A passport official appeared with a policewoman beside him. "My name is Megumi Yamada. I don't know you," I said quickly to justify myself. Jörg's face distorted in a grimace. "What's wrong with you?" No, this is Jörg, and he isn't wearing the uniform of a customs official; I'm not a criminal but rather a library patron. Frau Finder knows me to be an upstanding individual. My only problem is that I no longer have a passport. This is the only blemish on my character. How could I be arrested on such ridiculous grounds? "What's wrong with you? Is everything all right?" "I don't have a passport." Jörg burst out laughing. "You don't need to show a passport anymore. All you need is a ticket. That's all they check nowadays." "Even if I travel to Moscow?" "Well, for Moscow you would still need a passport. But why in the world would you want to go to Moscow?" "The Soviet government will bring me home." "The Soviet Union no longer exists. Don't you know that?" "Yes, I know, but what other country am I supposed to travel through to get home?" "If we both go home together, there's no country between here and there." "Where is here? Where is there?" I wasn't speaking any longer, I was braying. Frau Finder suggested that the three of us go out for scallops. First she would close the library, turn off the lights, and shut the windows. She announced these things with a dutiful expression. I was somewhat reassured that she was treating the turning off of lights as something just as important as the conversation that was to take place between Jörg and myself.

In the restaurant to which Frau Finder took us, she ordered a bottle of red wine for the three of us. I didn't want to drink any wine, only a sip to moisten my dry lips. But against my will I swallowed down the first glass in one gulp. Jörg refilled my glass. The wine tasted like a disagreeable insinuation. "You're drinking too fast," Jörg remarked as I gulped down the second glass. Frau Finder translated each of these sentences like a faithful echo. Back then in East Berlin, Jörg and I drank vodka. Now I was drinking wine staring at the very same face, and my rational faculties remained as clear as Evian.

Jörg coughed and said: "You ought to come back with me to Bochum and recuperate. There would also be the possibility of a therapeutic treatment." Frau Finder continued to translate into French what Jörg said in German.

The French language was only sounding familiar to me now because it was mediating a language, German, that felt even more foreign. "Therapy? I'm not sick. And anyway I don't want to disturb you. You have surely gotten married by now." Jörg understood these sentences and responded in a flash: "I was briefly married once, years ago, then quickly got divorced." Frau Finder went to wash her hands. Jörg's forehead neared mine, and his voice, taking on a familiar tone, whispered something in Russian. I couldn't recognize a single word of what he said.

"What are you living on? What is your profession? Why are you so thin?" I couldn't tell if it was Jörg asking me these questions or Frau Finder. The scallops were served, they lay on the plate like charred butterflies. "I have to remain in Paris. I have an important reason." A waiter with a lonely face wandered over, looking absent-mindedly out the window at a black car that had just pulled in and shut off its engine.

I said goodbye to Jörg. We made a date to meet the next day at Frau Finder's desk at the library. At home, I imagined what it would be like if I were to go to Bochum with Jörg. We would buy a wall calendar and tear off one page every day until the calendar was thin and the days piled in the wastepaper basket. Then we would buy a new calendar and then another, and one day I would convince him to travel to Saigon with me on vacation. From Marie's basement I would never be able to go to anywhere. So it would surely be better to return to Bochum. Marie would continue living alone. I couldn't abandon Marianne at *Place Vendôme*, though. She would have to come with me. Otherwise she would drink and drink and would soon die with her nameless diamonds in her hand. I couldn't let her die inside me.

Didn't you warn that young woman never to take on the role of a messenger? The diamonds are transported by the hands of women. Once they reach their new owner, the messenger is destroyed. You tell the young woman every-

thing you know even though she is your rival. The young
woman doesn't listen.

"Why don't you want to come with me?" Jörg asked if I had
a lover in Paris. "No, I don't have one. I don't want to leave
behind the Parisian movie theaters." Frau Finder laughed
before she translated. Jörg laughed too and looked relieved.
"You can see a movie anywhere in the world. That's why
they invented film. It's really ridiculous to refuse to leave a
city because of the cinemas." I didn't understand what he
meant. He became impatient, and Frau Finder placed her
hand on his thigh to calm him. "Every movie that is shown
in Paris is shown in Bochum as well." Frau Finder gave Jörg
a critical look, and he corrected his statement: "Well, not
every movie, but many of them."

When I left the Institute together with Jörg and wandered among the nocturnal bars, I was confused by the
scent of his jacket. I felt I was playing a part in a movie with
a plot unknown to me.

Chapter Twelve

Est, Ouest

It isn't chloroform making

my eyelids heavy. Who wouldn't fall asleep at a moment of
border crossing long anticipated in dreams?

Triton, tuna, Turkish freighters. The ocean's water is rock-
ing. The irresistible effect of film music. From the

high waves upon the screen your name suddenly appears. I
hold my breath. The name is a promise.

There was no *Ecran* in Bochum. Surely this city possessed a darkroom where my lonely retinas could make contact with your body. In the local newspaper, I found the "Movies" section. A new film of yours was scheduled to open the following week. "I'll go with you," Jörg said.

Russian and French intermingle in a parlor. A Frenchwoman who cannot speak Russian is sitting between two Russians who are speaking French. The Frenchwoman is named Marie—this Marie played not by you but by some other actress. Therefore I cannot call this figure Marie. I'll call her Sandrine, since this is the actress's name. The floor sways beneath the feet of the guests as they travel to the East on a ship.

Intellectuals with the obligatory piano and wineglasses. Even on a ship they insist on having the same fixtures as in their apartments. They are traveling back to the Russian soil they haven't set foot on in thirty years. My soil! An old man squats down and kisses the earth. One of the soldiers pulls him up disrespectfully and forces him to stand upright. The soul is a sort of potato if the earth is its mother.

Nocturnal and wet gleams the harbor of Odessa. A coarse, crackling voice is pouring out of the loudspeaker: the Soviet

Union welcomes the emigrants from the West. Someone steps out of line and is shot. "How awful," Jörg whispers in my ear.

A gigantic building filled with barren spaces and broken walls. In the next room, someone is screaming in fear; the footsteps in the corridor reverberate as in a prison. Sandrine, suspected of spying, is being interrogated. Alexei is advised to divorce her and marry a Soviet woman. Since he is unwilling to do this, his wife and son are sent with him to Kiev as punishment. Sandrine has never in her life shared an apartment with five families. There is only a single bathtub for everyone, and one kitchen. An inebriated man with a fluttering shirt staggers into the kitchen and teases Sandrine, who, distracted by him, drops the plate she is drying on the floor. The plate shatters, laughter erupts. A woman with an ignorant, aggressively painted face gives a spiteful laugh. "I'm sure Kiev is a gorgeous city, but that's not what they're showing us," I whisper in Jörg's ear.

"This is horrible," Jörg murmurs at my side. Perhaps he has already begun to identify with the character Alexei. The film is drilling these characters into our hearts. "Jörg, you aren't a doctor, you can't play the piano, you are not Alexei!" My ironic remarks have no effect. Jörg is Alexei and is suffering at having to share such close quarters with simple people. He has fallen into the screen's trap. The walls are broken, the pipes in the bathroom rusted.

Close quarters? Really? Do you feel cramped? Do you think an apartment like this is fit only for simple folk? In the house where I was born, we lived in even tighter quarters. Do you consider me one of these simple folk?

"No, not at all," Jörg said right away, "but we can't simply join in the workers' lives, I mean, we can't even bear the workers, that's really something we should honestly admit." I asked: "Are you not a worker? Every day you work like a slave for your boss. You're scarcely allowed to make any decisions at all. Are you really not a worker?"

There is someone behind the screen who is trying to convince Jörg and the other moviegoers of something. Jörg, you are something better than a worker, Jörg, you are a free man. Who is saying this? The writer? The director? The producer? What are the names of these cowards who are hiding behind the screen? The only thing I want is for you to finally make your appearance on the screen and change the plot, which displeases me.

Unbefitting, Sandrine thinks at first. We are not accustomed to living under poor conditions. It must be a misunderstanding that we've wound up here. We have to leave this place as quickly as possible. How unjust that the family of a doctor should have to live like workers, Sandrine thinks. How much longer until we can go back again? An outrage. Sandrine is furious—she is not permitted to return. Her French passport is taken from her and torn into pieces, and she is struck in the face. Her lips bleed and swell. She is to remain there and become a worker. There is no other interpretation.

"Get out of here!" I say to the cinematographic current trying to carry me off with it. Leave me alone. I don't want to be carried off. But it was difficult to maintain a distance from the images. They swept me away with them, wanting to drown me. Why was I, a free human being, not allowed to turn off the images when I wished or at least correct them? I wished to experience boredom, for this would at least entail the individual freedom not to take part. If I fell asleep in my seat, the film would have been better for me. I had to remain awake, though, to wait for you.

A simple woman: this is how the woman sharing the apartment with Sandrine's family describes herself. I am a simple woman. How did the filmmaker find this face, which really does embody the type of the flawlessly simple woman? Perhaps she was operated on before the shoot. It cannot be possible for a person to look so typical. It is possible that the camera shows the woman only from one particular angle to make her appear typical. Perhaps it isn't even necessary to operate on a face because the retina is secretly being operated on during the screening of the film.

Choirs are rehearsing on the stage of a theater. In the dressing room, Sandrine is ironing a dancer's *rubashka*. Ironing is now her profession. And while her work dress doesn't suit her, her unfriendly colleague wears the very same dress like a second skin. Even if only for reasons of fashion, the upper class must remain on top, the film is saying, the upper class should never wear workers' clothing, the workers must do the working.

As a swimmer, Sasha has nothing on but swim trunks. He is wearing neither an office suit nor a military uniform nor a work shirt. For reasons of fashion, his future is open.

Day after day Sasha trains in the cold river. He was on the team that trained in the warm indoor pool, but when his performance began to wane, the trainer kicked him out. "You drink too much!" "I'm having a rough time. My grandmother just died." "Mine too. That's no reason to get lazy. You're off the team! We can send only the very best to compete in the West. They despise us there. That's why we must win." Sasha's parents were liquidated long ago as enemies of the state. Later the same thing happened to the grandmother who had raised him.

The characters in this film spoke both French and Russian. I pretended that I understood a great deal linguistically. The German subtitles drifting across the lower edge of the screen like autumn leaves did not disturb me.

"Did you know things were like that in the Soviet Union?" Jörg asked. I was beginning to understand more and more of the words Jörg said to me. What I couldn't grasp was what exactly he meant by them. My counter-questions remained unspoken in my head. What do you mean by "like that"? Do you mean that every older female department head in the Soviet Union sexually harassed a good-looking young doctor? Do you mean that ...

... ice cream from Kiev tasted good to a Parisian child? Sandrine's little son eats ice cream in a boat on the river. The simple man rowing the boat asks him if it tastes good. On the shore, Sandrine stands watching with an earnest face as Sasha swims against the current. He feels the woman's expectant gaze on his skin. I hate the unambiguous language of images. They're supposed to tell me that Sandrine loves Sasha and Sasha loves Sandrine. No member of the audience is allowed to think anything different. One can at most allow oneself individual shades of interpretation, for example when Jörg says: "To Sandrine, Sasha embodies the energy a person needs to reach freedom. That's why she loves him." "So what?" I reply, two words I can pronounce fluently. "So what?" Sasha's supple skin is protecting his burden, his heavy muscles, from the world outside. Sandrine smears white fat ...

... on his back before he leaps into the river. She smears and smears; she is already perfectly familiar with his skin before she touches it for the first time in the bedroom. And the beautiful actress who is not entangled in any love story and will remain free until the end ...

... still does not appear. I am waiting for you, the one I know so well, the one who still does not know me. Alexei sleeps with a female functionary in order to save his skin politically, and Sandrine throws him out of the room. The neighbor, the simple woman in a nightgown, offers him a cigarette as he stands helplessly in the corridor. He is permitted to eat bread with her, read the newspaper, and sleep with her.

"No," I say aloud. "What?" Jörg asks in bewilderment. "She's the actress who stopped the train to Paris for me that night." Finally you've appeared on the screen—a stage actress arriving from France to perform a play by Victor Hugo. "I have come out of ideological conviction," you say. Therefore you have to speak with ordinary people; you don't want to participate in the staged official dinner. You have come to us out of ideological conviction. What ideology? The ideology of Victor Hugo? He was the cult figure of Caodaism, but as far as I know these teachings were unknown in France. What do you believe in? Your costume is a fusion between reptiles and flesh-eating plants. Gemstones glitter in your labia. Like a …

… an angel from *Sieben Planeten* you stand onstage, exactly as on that day beside the train tracks in Bochum. What freedom did you mean to promise me that day? Gabrielle is your name in this movie. Sandrine hurries into the changing room after the performance and asks Gabrielle to help her.

The Danube is calling Sasha. He has been nominated for the international competition in Vienna. "You must win— only sports can win over the people in the West. And don't get into any trouble." He is being encouraged and warned. His departure is prevented at the last moment: in his bag they found a letter that Sandrine had written to her sister in Paris.

I'm fine here, don't worry about me, Mama, says Sandrine's little boy. He isn't lying. He has other children to play with, children he runs giggling with through the building. The boy sits beside Sasha, who makes a paper airplane for him in a quiet park. Even the so-called simple workers have plenty of time for him. They give him ice cream, play with him. He plays, learns, eats, sleeps, and forgets what things were like before. It becomes more and more incomprehensible to him that life in Kiev is a catastrophe in his mother's eyes.

Sasha has been sent to Odessa to purify his heart in a training camp because he's been polluted by Sandrine. He secretly decides to leave the country for the free world no matter what—Turkey to start. A Greek captain is willing to transport him on his freighter for money. Then on the day of departure the captain refuses. Something has happened that has resulted in increased security measures. Sasha, who doesn't want to give up his plan, tells the captain he will meet the freighter out in the ocean. He'll have to swim five hours to get there. He leaps from the cliff and swims through the water, which is gradually darkening. Somewhere in the night he is supposed to find the ship. This is the climax of the film. Should I allow it to entrance me? The music forces me to swim along with him. The men's chorus sings melancholy Slavic melodies. In between we hear lighthearted Siberian dance rhythms that have a military ring but are still cheery enough to dance to. The music accompanies the loneliness of the swimmer, lending it a generous portion of romanticism and drama, tries to tug me along to reach the mainland of freedom.

Frozen months and years in the story of a lifetime. Sandrine's stay in the labor camp lasts five years. She emerges with skin white as wax, engraved with deep furrows. The camera holds for a long time on the wrinkles around her eyes. I wonder if these wrinkles have been painted on or if they are real wrinkles that are ordinarily hidden beneath make-up. Whatever the case they are nothing other than shadows on the screen, which remains smooth the entire time. On the day of Sandrine's release, Alexei and their son come to pick her up. She cries because of the smell she is unable to remove from her body.

And the son, who is already taller than his mother, keeps his lips closed for the most part, saying only the most necessary things. Sometimes he cries in secret. Otherwise he sits bolt upright before the Party assembly on the television. In front of the TV screen, his eyes become hollow. "Did you also see programs like that when you were a child?" Jörg asked me on the way home. We didn't have a television, I replied. At home he opened the bottommost drawer of his dresser and pulled out a manuscript. "I kept this ...

...because it belonged to you. I never threw it away because I thought the past must be preserved. Can you still remember what it is?" Yellowed pages covered in writing from top to bottom. A childish script. Russian. "Don't you recognize it?" he asks. I read the mysteriously familiar lines: "Dear comrades in Berlin, today I would like to tell you about our country, the history of our country, how it was destroyed and how it nevertheless has remained whole because we have all applied ourselves seriously to reading and writing, just as our former President Ho Chi Minh always emphasized in his speeches."

I dropped the sheets of paper in horror. Jörg's lips were poised to laugh, then suddenly froze when he saw me. He wanted me to laugh along with him, to laugh at my own youthful folly, my inhibited infatuation with a pipe dream, wanted me to flush it from my head and fall into his arms so as to become part of his living room, which was dominated by the color of natural wood and the black of digital technology. On the large, flat screen, a healthy and relaxed-looking moderator with a colorful necktie was speaking.

Canada sounds like an ordinary noun that might mean, for example, something like "happiness." The entire world should become Canada, according to Jörg. Sasha is free as long as he is exposed to mortal danger in the Black Sea. Once he arrives in France, he is no longer free. The authorities decide what will become of this small, unimportant refugee. He is not allowed to remain in France. Canada takes him. What good news. He is given a new passport which helps him forget everything that happened to him during his childhood. Go to Canada! Canada is a promise. Sasha, though, doesn't want to be sent off to this compulsory happiness—he wants to stay in France and wait for

Sandrine or, failing that, return to Kiev. "Are you mad?" "I expected more from freedom," Sasha says and slits his wrists. His hands would have drowned in a small washbasin in the hotel room if Gabrielle hadn't come.

"That's just stupid, he never learned what to do with freedom," Jörg remarked. "Naïve Sasha thinks he can immediately get everything from us for free. It's what everyone from over there thinks, and it really gets on my nerves," Jörg continued. "Why should Sasha get everything when I still haven't gotten anything?" Now Jörg's competition is the champion swimmer.

Tango in Sofia. So that is Sofia. My second time seeing the movie, I recognized the city by its Alexander Nevsky Cathedral. The business travelers sit together in a ballroom, toasting Russian-Bulgarian friendship. Alexei and Sandrine are dancing the tango with its nostalgic bourgeois footwork. Their son observes his dancing parents with a thoughtful look because he knows something. The second time around, I too know what he knows. A tango is always being danced for the last time, in Sofia, in Indochina, and elsewhere.

"Ho Chi Minh no longer exists, like Honecker," said Jörg. He was attempting to wrap cilantro, bean sprouts, and shrimp in rice paper. A friend of his who'd spent a lot of time in Southeast Asia had taught him to make spring rolls. He wanted to do something nice for me. "Don't roll everything up together! You're getting it all mixed up!" His spring rolls were making me more furious than grateful. "And stop talking about my childhood!" These last words I actually didn't say out loud. I quietly left the house. My legs only knew a single direction. The tickets were always made of the same gray recycled paper. I knew exactly how the movie ended, since I'd already seen it twice. It ended with a text containing the name "Gorbachev." His name put an end to the years of imprisonment. My life, too, had once almost ended with a quite similar name. I knew that the film was trying to end with a period, a bit of punctuation with some finality about it, not wanting to let us down with a comma. But then again, why not let us down? This third viewing was necessary for me because I wished to study a few important images more closely without Jörg's commentary. For example, Sandrine's shoes. She leaves the hotel in Sofia with her son, gets into a taxi in which Gabrielle is already waiting for her. In the taxi, Gabrielle gives Sandrine a new French passport and a capitalist coat. Sandrine puts it on, gets out of the taxi, and with her son walks down the sidewalk leading to the entrance to the French embassy. Sandrine shows the Bulgarian guard her passport; the guard finds nothing suspicious about it, though his eyes pursue her from behind. Something isn't right about this woman, he thinks, but he has nothing to fix his suppositions on.

Finally his gaze reaches her shoes, a kind of lace-up boot. The boots must have counted as Communist footwear, for the guard suddenly gives a shout and runs after her. Stop! Stay right where you are! Sandrine keeps going, running faster and faster, lurching and stumbling, but she doesn't fall down because her son is holding her firmly and running beside her while Gabrielle blocks the guard's way.

Quickly Sandrine and her son leap onto the grounds of the French embassy. The old laced boots that can no longer hold the body of the woman upright stay on her feet. Sandrine faints at the foot of a curving staircase with a red carpet. The next day Sandrine sleeps in an automobile as it crosses the border.

"You're still never quite present when I talk to you," Jörg sighs. "Where were you today? At the movies. Again? Why do you go to see the same film a hundred times in a row? I don't know. And you still haven't bought yourself new shoes."

So what? Why should I? You should think of your appearance. Just look at those ...

... disgusting broken sandals made of automobile tires. Surely you've noticed by now:

•

It was nothing other than

misery there,

nothing other than

a hideous fraud! Realize this

and finally

forget

the images of the past. Yes. I will forget them, but to do that, I'll have to poke my eyes out with the second hand of the clock.

Chapter Thirteen

Dancer in the Dark

Selma lived in Berlin for three years before emigrating to the U.S., where she was later condemned to death. Emigrating from Prague to Berlin wasn't difficult. She visited an aunt who owned a flower shop in a district called Pankow, then didn't leave Berlin a week later as she promised to do when she first crossed the border, but instead stayed on for a month, and then another month, and then a year, and so on. At first she helped her aunt in the shop and the kitchen, then she got a job in a warehouse where she checked the deliveries. Later she got a room in a shared apartment. This three-bedroom apartment was already occupied by Selma's cousin and a young couple. In front of the dark-brown building there was a little garden with thin grass and flashy buttercups. Sometimes a neighbor woman would be standing there with her little dog. The dog would bark at Selma, his voice sounding threatening, though he was hardly larger than a tomcat. The woman with the dog was delicately built, her almost gray hair that used to be blond was tied in the back, and she wore tinted glasses. Selma learned from her cousin that this woman was blind. Selma's roommates secretly referred to her as the "lady with the lapdog." One evening in 1988, a foreign girl had been attacked near Alexanderplatz by a group of teenagers. The lady with the lapdog, who coincidentally was walking beside the girl, had tried to stop the youths. They then attacked her as well. The girl later died of a stab wound, while the woman was blinded.

On the street where Selma lived, there were several grand villas, most of them empty. Their windows, though, were always clean, the gardens well tended. This quiet street led to a larger road which was the scene of normal everyday life. A row of gray apartment buildings with a supermarket in the middle, and beside it a parking lot and a bus stop where an overcrowded bus stopped every ten minutes.

On Saturday, Selma wanted to go to a café at the far end of the street that had just opened two weeks before. She knew that young people who looked like actors went there to drink *café au lait*. She wanted to sit among them. She knew she was too shy to speak to a stranger, but it was still her dream to work in a theater. When she left the house, the blind woman was standing on the grass with her dog. The dog barked and jumped at Selma because he wasn't leashed. The blind woman asked her forgiveness, held the dog by its collar, and asked Selma if she had time to help her read some letters. The social workers hadn't come by for a week—supposedly they all had the flu. Selma couldn't say no; she climbed the steps to the building together with the woman. The blind woman's apartment was on the uppermost floor. There was no name plate on the door. The apartment smelled of tropical fruit, but there was no fruit on the table, just a heap of letters that was larger than the dog. It had surely been more than a week since the social workers' last visit. Perhaps no one had ever come to see her, Selma thought and picked up a letter from the top of the pile. A French stamp was on the envelope. The woman moved comfortably about the kitchen, put on water for coffee, and asked Selma to sit down at the table. That's a lot of letters, do you really want me to read all of them to you? I'd like to help you, but it will take a long time to read all of them. The blind woman shook her right hand in negation and said that actually there was only a single letter she was eager to find and read. Then she asked Selma where she was born. Selma thought she could discern a very faint, unfamiliar accent in the woman's speech. In Prague, Selma replied, and then asked the woman the same thing. She smiled, relieved, as if she'd been waiting the whole time for this question, and replied proudly: in Saigon. Selma asked again: Where? In Saigon. Selma fell silent, embarrassed, observing the woman's European-looking face. One could have blond streaks dyed in gray hair, but were these eyes, nose, and cheeks Vietnamese? Then it occurred to Selma that perhaps this woman was a descendant of French nationals who had remained behind in Vietnam. Are you of French descent? No, all my ancestors were from Asia. I spent ten years living in Paris that were not my fault. Fault? It wasn't what I wanted, I mean. I thought Paris was wonderful, but it was a misunderstanding if not an accident. After my eye operation failed I moved to Berlin. Did you have the operation in Paris? No, in Bochum, but I didn't want to stay there. Berlin was my point of departure. How do you mean? The blind woman got up as if she didn't want to talk any more, and with perfect aim poured the boiling water into the filter cone. The dark liquid slowly dripped into the glass pot.

Do you know what I find so charming about this building? The radiator pipes, which sometimes play percussion. Do you like listening to them too? The woman waited for Selma's response. Selma was listening. She knew the sound, her roommates sometimes complained about it. This building is in need of renovation! There are holes everywhere! How can they ask so much rent for a hole in the wall that's full of holes!

You know, vision is a gap, a crevice—it isn't that you have a view through this gap, rather, vision itself is this gap, and at the point where it is you can't see anything at all. It no longer bothers me to be blind. The only problem is that people immediately want to start telling me their life stories when they hear about my blindness. I don't want to hear any more life stories, I don't want to hear much of anything, not even music interests me anymore, the only interesting thing left are sounds, if that.

If I could see, I would work in a factory. The sound of a screw that falls to the floor and rolls back and forth, tracing a semi-circle. Thin metal plates that are being bent create hauntingly fluctuating sounds. A hammer strikes the head of a nail. The water gushes out of a big faucet and strikes the bottom of a bucket. A forklift drives between wooden crates. An oversized sliding door opens with a grating sound. Factory labor is inhuman, Selma replied, I don't want to work in a factory, I want to work in a theater. Even the theater is inhuman, the woman replied calmly, and continued: still, I enjoy going to the theater, and enjoy the movies even more, especially now that I can concentrate on the voices and the finger movements of my friend. My friend Kathy, you see, translates the images into finger language and taps them on my palm. My hand is my screen, and Kathy's fingers are the authors. I have no doubt that she changes things in the story she doesn't like. In a film without images, most people are merely footsteps. They ramble through sleepless nights, are chased, race through alleyways, descend spiral staircases, or hide in basements. Sometimes Kathy draws an open circle in my hand like the letter "C," or her finger draws a straight line and then a semicircle, which is the letter "D." I cannot see the face of the woman who is dancing, at least not the way a policeman can see and identify a face. Faces that look like passport photos no longer mean anything to me. I would like to see the dance, I mean, the strange, meaningless motions that people make.

And where does Kathy live? Selma asked out of curiosity. She had never before seen the blind woman in the company of anyone at all. I don't know where she is now. But when I go to the movies, the woman said, she always sits beside me.